HEART OF THE WALKER

BOOK TWO IN THE WALKER SERIES

Jenifer

CORALEE JUNE

Have Heart

xoxo,

Coralee June

Created with Vellum

 Created with Vellum

For Amanda. I'm always amazed by the things you don't find embarrassing about me. Thank you for not thinking I'm weird. I mean, we both know I'm weird, but you accept it, and that makes me happy.

CHAPTER ONE

Josiah, Two years ago

I shouldn't like how Ashleigh blushes whenever I'm near, but some sick part of me does. I can't help but watch her with morbid fascination as she serves my favorite dinner—roasted chicken and potatoes with caramelized carrots. I suspect she made it because she overheard Father and me fighting again this morning. It was our usual row. He has high expectations for his predecessor, yet I have no desire to follow in his clumsy, corrupt footsteps.

Nothing about Ashleigh is supposed to draw me in. She isn't particularly spectacular in any sense of the word. Her appearance is mostly plain, and her status is definitely beneath mine, but I can't help but feel eager and curious when she exhibits little rebellious displays of affection. Like how she made my favorite dish tonight when Father requested venison.

Ashleigh is supposed to be worth nothing more to me than the flashy furniture in this very dining room. Walkers are only procured by wealthy families seeking to impress equally wealthy enemies; a decorative fixture in our lavish home. Ashleigh is a daily reminder that our family can afford the vaccine that many others can't. At least, that's what I've been conditioned to think, and yet I feel that there's something more to this little Walker.

Over the last year, she stopped seeing me as her childhood hero and started seeing me as something else, and damn—I liked it. The adoration in her smile made me feel uncomfortable and on edge. I hated that I sought out any and every opportunity to steal moments with the hazel-eyed woman with wild hair and a tame heart. My eyes found themselves glued to her whenever she entered the room, and I enjoyed listening to her hum while she baked, the sound a stark bright melody against the hopelessness of the manor. She glows with acceptance and optimism despite her dismal place in this fucked up world.

Ashleigh rarely complains, and her complacent moods are frightfully alluring.

When Ashleigh was younger, I politely entertained the worship she so plainly bestowed upon me, but this new development has me conflicted. Her curves and desire to please wholly absorb me into her orbit, and her complete, consuming devotion makes my fascination grow daily.

At best, Ashleigh is a distraction. At worst, she is something Father can use against me. I've been groomed as his successor as Governor of the Galla Providence since I was able to speak, and someone like Ashleigh is exactly what he would force me to stay away from.

I hate him.

Father notices her naive yet addicting allure, too. He leers whenever she bends to serve our dinner, and I notice how his grey eyes seek the plush lift of her chest in the window between her dirty dress and freckled skin. He follows her movements with the intense focus of a predator.

I don't want him to see or guess just how much Ashleigh has burrowed herself into my existence. This peculiar fascination with my little Walker is disastrous, but I can't help but feel somewhat attached. Our connection is a burning train destined to derail and destroy us both.

I continue about my dinner in silence, trying to work through how Ashleigh carved out a blackened piece of my dead heart and miraculously pulsed life back through it.

CHAPTER TWO

Ashleigh, Present Day

The General Store was buzzing with chatty and overly curious customers, providing a constant yet monotonous noise in the over-crowded space. It was my first official day, and citizens of the Dormas Providence were supremely curious about the Walker that warranted a rescue mission from the entire Dormas Leadership Council.

Their curious gazes loomed at me over the wooden, dusty shelves. Not one for being used to attention, I found their nosiness to be endearing but annoying.

Lois and Mark Caverly, the General Store owners, thrived upon the attention they received from hiring me to be the Baker in their quaint store. They resolved to introduce me to every single patron that graced their front steps, even going as far as to wave in walking pedestrians to take a look at the Walker that stumbled into the Dormas Leadership Council's favored eye.

Lois pointedly told anyone willing to listen that I was the daughter she never had. She even tried marrying me off to at least seven mine workers that stopped by to indulge in a muffin on their morning walk to work. She was harmless but thrived upon the curious energy of her customers. Despite all of this, I preferred her intrusive company to the self-pity and loneliness I experienced while moping around Black Manor. Keeping busy kept me from crying.

It's been one month since Josiah forcefully plucked me from the Dormas Summer Solstice and used me as a pawn in emperorLackley's political games. Since then, I've spent every waking moment trying to heal from the emotional scars left behind by Josiah's betrayal and his confusing motives.

Most of my time of sadness was spent in a grueling, cleaning frenzy. I scrubbed every square inch of the Black Manor. Eventually, Cyler's patience broke, and he begged me to start my job as the Baker at the

General Store. I guess a month of crying and cleaning was wearing him thin.

I spent most my morning hiding from customers and becoming acclimated with the dusty and virtually unused bakery. I already had a few orders and needed to get to work. The wooden countertops were splintered, yet usable, but the oven wasn't level, which would be a big problem. I sent a quick message to Kemper asking him to add it to the long list of repairs needed in the Providence. As usual, in his perpetually considerate nature, Kemper replied back with, "Whatever you need, Ash." My cheeks flamed with appreciation, and Lois' curious stare appraised me with a knowing smirk.

Over the last month, I've become more comfortable with voicing my needs, despite my sadness. Perhaps it was everyone's willingness to please, or maybe I was evolving outside of my Walker mindset. Either way, I've come to heavily rely on Cyler, Maverick, Kemper, Jacob, Patrick, and even Huxley. I enjoyed the comfort that they gave me, and even more, I enjoyed learning to assert my independence, yet seek help when needed.

Cyler placed my first official order. He decided that the Solstice Festival cake didn't *technically* count, since no one was able to enjoy it thanks to

Josiah's little kidnapping stunt. Two chocolate cakes —one for him and one for the rest of our little makeshift family—sat upon a cooling rack by the window, and I beamed with pride. Cyler's encouragement and confidence in me was contagious. Apparently, once word went around that Cyler Black, fearless leader of Dormas, was ordering cakes from me, others promptly placed identical orders with equal enthusiasm.

I made quick work of mixing the thick batter for my other orders and pouring it into various cake pans. I made a note of what utensils and gadgets the Bakery lacked, then migrated to my other workstation and sat down. I started the peaceful task of painting a little wooden doll with a wild and crooked smile

There were about three dozen children total in Dormas, and Lois Caverly recently decided to add a toy section in her store to accommodate the growing number of children. Once Lois learned of my artistic whims, she promptly decided that Mark would carve them, I would paint them, and Lois would happily coordinate both of our efforts while she sipped lemonade and gossiped with visitors.

I was busy painting when the shop bell rang throughout the store, indicating that another customer had arrived. I put the finishing touches on the doll's face, then nervously turned to greet the shop's new guest. I wasn't in the mood for another matchmaking attempt by Lois. She was determined to have me married off by sunset, and the overabundance of men in this town allowed for many opportunities to embarrass me. However, instead of being greeted by another nosy stranger, Jacob's playful chocolate eyes met mine.

"Hey, sweetheart, Lois is putting you to work, I see." He observed me with a smile while noting the paint that covered my dress and hands before carefully hugging me in greeting. He kept his chest a good six inches away from me while his hands loosely patted my upper back. It was rare that I finished a project without getting splatters of different colors on my nose and in my hair. After a few mishaps and ruined shirts, the guys learned to proceed with caution.

Jacob then inspected my batch of toys with a squinted eye and mock seriousness. I watched in amusement as he dusted off a few of the toys with dried paint and polished them with the corner of his sleeve. Since my involuntary visit with emperorLackley, I hadn't seen Jacob much, mostly because Jules was back and had taken up permanent residence in her old bedroom. I was forced to bounce from room to room, depending on who had night-guard duty. Jacob opted to work most nights to avoid her, but as a result, the only time I had with him was when he snuck around the house while Jules was either away or indulging in one of her frequent cat naps.

Lois rounded the corner with her arms overflowing with more projects for me to do, but nearly dropped them all when she eyed Jacob's impressive form playfully scrutinizing our hard work.

"Oh! He-hello! Jacob, it's so good to see you. How's our new schoolhouse coming along?" Her wrinkled cheeks reddened while she shifted the unpainted toys to one arm and straightened her long grey braid with the other. I grinned at her reaction to him. It was easy to get flustered around Jacob—around all of them; it was like staring into the sun.

"It's going great, Mrs. Caverly. I just received another shipment of supplies. It should be ready within a couple of weeks. Kemper's got us all working on it. We might even get Dormas' resident artist to paint a mural on the outside wall," he said. He threw a flirtatious wink my way, causing both Lois and I to sigh. He knew the effect he had on women, and he reveled in it.

"What brings you here?" I asked Jacob. I liked

having my playful friend around, but it was definitely out of the ordinary. I've been on edge ever since Lackley's forced deal, as well as worried that more of Dormas would end up exploited under the pressure of the Empire's thumb.

"I came to pick you up," he said before eyeing Lois with a polite yet intentional glare, giving me the impression that there was something he wanted to tell me without an audience. Lois inferred this, too, because she quickly got the hint and excused herself with an awkward bow that left Jacob and I feeling secondhand embarrassment on her behalf. I assumed that she would migrate behind one of the shop's many shelves to try and eavesdrop, so I pulled Jacob by the elbow, farther away .

"We're traveling to the Deadlands tonight," he said in a low tone while stepping closer to me. He smelled of soap and fresh air. Jacob crossed his arms over his chest and looked around the room for eavesdroppers. The easygoing playfulness of before rolled like mist over the tone of the room before disappearing into an ominous cloud between us.

"But why? The only thing in the Deadlands are Scavengers," I insisted while scrunching my eyebrows down in confusion.

"Exactly. Huxley was able to coordinate a

meeting with one of the more open-minded Scavenger tribes. They requested that the entire Dormas Leadership Council be in attendance, and the *majority* of us decided it was best that you come with us."

My mouth gaped open in shock. Scavengers were wild and feral people that refused to move to the Walker Zones when the vaccine for X was first created. They were fearless, fierce, and a major source of trouble for Providences on the outer rim of the Empire. Back in Galla, I remember watching the reports late at night after Master and Mistress Stonewell were asleep. They showed videos of pale beings with intricate scarring on their backs, and blood running down their faces. They were known for looting and tearing down entire Providences.

"Are we sure that's a good idea?" I asked while rubbing the bridge of my nose.

Jacob looked at me with a grim expression while he ran his hand over his caramel chin. His deeply furrowed brow sunk, and I knew that he, too, was unsure about this meeting.

"We'll be fine, Ash. I won't let anything happen to that pretty face of yours." He chuckled before pinching my cheek in an unconvincing friendly gesture that made me feel like a whining, insolent child. "Hux has a *special* relationship with this particular tribe," he added in, what I assumed, was a reassuring tone, but instead, more fear coursed through me.

"It's not me I'm worried about." This new family was incredibly important to me. I was more worried that they were blindly rushing into a dangerous situation.

Jacob stepped closer towards me and wrapped his toned arms around my small frame in a comforting hug. I held my hands away from his defined back to avoid getting paint on his blue shirt. "You're always worrying about the wrong things" he whispered.

"So you admit it, we have reason to worry?" I searched his expression, but Jacob didn't respond.

Lois loudly coughed when re-entering the room, and I removed myself from Jacob's comforting hold while willing the blush on my cheeks to evaporate. I cleaned up my workstation while Jacob maintained a polite conversation with the flustered Mrs. Lois. I noticed her twirling the end of her braid around her dainty finger while she laughed at whatever he said. Once through, Jacob and I said our goodbyes and made our way to the train station.

We walked in comfortable, yet foreboding

silence, neither one of us willing to discuss the Scavenger meeting. Both our hands swung with purposeful carelessness at our sides, and occasionally our knuckles brushed, causing tingles of anticipation to move up and down my arm. A part of me wanted to grab the tips of Jacob's calloused fingers, but each time courage boiled up within me, self-preservation and the reminder of Jules' crime stopped me.

I repeated my usual mantra to keep from blurring the lines between us: *Not mine. Not mine. Not mine* . Our fingers continued to collide until finally, Jacob huffed and grabbed my hand. His thumb carefully caressed my wrist, and I enjoyed the feel of him. It was reassuring to know that he, too, felt this unspoken desire to touch.

Jacob remained silent while we walked hand in hand, neither of us willing to say out loud what we were thinking. The sound of my beating heart drowned out all the thunderous doubts floating about my mind. It felt like I was in a continuous cycle of falling and standing back up.

Just as we were about to arrive at the train station, a breathy but shrill voice stopped us in our tracks. Jacob immediately dropped my hand and whirled around to address the interloper on our little moment, and I felt a sudden vacancy at his departure.

"Oh Jacob, I'm just so glad I caught you. One of the shopkeepers mentioned that you and *the Walker* are going to the train station," Jules panted out while jogging towards us in her ostentatious heels that sunk in the soft dirt each time she took a step. She wore a thin black dress that showed off the outline of her ivory bra, with a plunging neckline and an opened back. As usual, she looked perfect, and I absentmindedly ran my calloused hands over the wrinkles in my modest tan dress with pockets and splatters of paint across the chest.

Once closer, Jules threw a sneer at me before fixing a fake smile back in place upon her porcelain face. The house dynamics had changed drastically since Jules moved back in to Black Manor. Charged tension bounced between the home's walls like balls of electricity. We no longer had family dinner, and everyone avoided her like she had X. Jules was an ornery combination of persistent and snobby. I tried to provide her with politeness, but she made it clear that I wasn't worthy of her attention or kindness, which left me tiptoeing around the manor in an effort to avoid her.

"Ash and I are going on a picnic," Jacob briefly

explained while tossing a purposeful glare towards me. His intensity indicated that he didn't want Jules to know about our trip to the Deadlands.

"How odd," she observed. "Did the Walker not prepare you a basket?" Jules twirled her glossy raven hair around her thin finger. "I'd love to join you both. The fresh air is simply lovely today, don't you think, Jacob?" She then took a step closer to him, and I felt my teeth begin to grind against one another with impatience.

I was never one to handle conflict particularly well, and Jules was like a steamroller; she crashed through whatever got in the way of what she wanted—consequences be damned.

"I was hoping for some alone time with Ash," Jacob said with more force than necessary. Once again, his calloused hand found mine, and I felt reassured by his contact .

"I see," Jules scoffed. "I wasn't under the impression that you both had formed that sort of relationship. I guess she's moved on from her dear Josiah then." Jules gave a calculating smile. "Well, I'll be heading back home, then. I do truly hope to get some alone time too, Jacob. I—I'd like to talk to you." Jules gave him a sad look before pushing her perfectly styled hair over her shoulder. She turned around and began walking with a forced, sensual sway along the dirt road back towards the Black Manor, leaving Jacob and me in an awkward silence.

"I'm sorry, Ashleigh," Jacob rasped.

"You don't have anything to apologize for," I replied as we continued our trek to the train station. "Jules is very persistent."

"There was a time when she and I were best friends." His voice held a note of sadness that made my heart thud with an echoing pain. "I wish we could go back to that. It would be so much easier if I loved her back."

I observed Jacob and noticed his slumped shoulders and bowed head. Having Jules back in Dormas was wearing him down in ways that I couldn't understand, and I had been too self-absorbed lately to help him. I sensed that Jacob questioned his place here, as well as worried that Jules' persistence would further tarnish their group dynamic.

"You can't force yourself to love someone, Jacob," I gently told him.

"Are you speaking from experience?" He guided me around a large muddy puddle in the middle of the road.

"Not exactly," I muttered. I focused on the splatter of ruby paint that kissed my thumb, and how

it looked beautiful against Jacob's brown skin. I struggled to formulate into words the thoughts that have
been plaguing me for the past few weeks. "It's more
like," I began, "I have to force myself *not* to love
someone. I have to remind myself that he doesn't
deserve my heart."

Jacob paused for a moment as if allowing my
words to sink in. He stopped walking and pulled
me close.

"He doesn't, you know." Jacob stepped closer to
me. He brushed my curls behind my ear and left a
lingering palm against my neck that felt hot and
made my skin buzz with anticipation. "A heart like
yours should be cherished, sweetheart."

Before I could respond, a joyful holler startled us
and pulled me from our intense conversation. I
looked down the road and saw Cyler eying us with
amusement.

"I was wondering what was taking you both so
long!" He joked in his usual gruff tone that I had
grown to adore since my time in Dormas. Cyler was
wearing midnight denim pants that clung tightly to
his muscular frame and an oversized black t-shirt that
still showed off his impressive muscles. His shoulder-
length hair was wavy and wild, and his light scruff

framed a broad smile. He stepped around Jacob and enveloped me in a crushing and delightful hug.

"Hey, babe," he mumbled against the thick curls of my hair before inhaling deeply. "You always smell like cake." He chuckled to himself, and the deep sound brushed against me in a subtle tickle that made me shiver. I giggled and squeezed him back while rising on my tiptoes. "Jacob was hoarding you all to himself when we've got important stuff to do!" Cyler joked.

The reminder of these 'important things' made my stomach drop and all lightheartedness fade away. We were headed to the Deadlands to secure an alliance with some of the most deadly and wild people in the entire Empire.

"Babe, don't look at me like that. This'll be easy!" Cyler boomed.

I wanted to voice my concerns but instead comfortably settled into the crook of Cyler's muscular arm. I chose to ignore the all-encompassing fear and enjoy my walk with him and Jacob towards the train station.

_____

CHAPTER THREE

C yler and Jacob kept the conversation light while we walked, and I sensed that they wanted to alleviate my concerns and distract me from the meeting ahead. I debated on asking to stay behind, but quickly extinguished that fleeting thought when I realized it would mean allowing the men I'd grown to care about travel into danger without me. Besides, I was a bit curious about the Scavenger way of life.

When we arrived at the station, Patrick, Huxley, Kemper, and Maverick were unloading various boxes from the cargo trolley. If it weren't for Cyler's purposeful strides, as well as the constant reminder that things needed to stay platonic between the seven of us, I might have stopped to appreciate the view.

Patrick and Huxley lifted heavy crates with ease while Kemper bit the end of a pencil and checked off items on the shipping order. Maverick took heaping gulps of water, and I watched as droplets trickled down his defined chin and neck. They worked seamlessly together.

Cyler's booming greeting got everyone's attention, and each of the guys rewarded me with smoldering smiles that made my mouth go dry. I licked my lips and noticed Cyler's eyes zero in on the movement of my tongue. He slowly raised his eyebrows at me before inspecting a pile of crates off to the left of the train. The guys seemed happy and in their element, but I noticed a thoughtful air about them that made my anxiety rekindle.

"Hey, Ash!" Patrick yelled while jumping off the cargo trolley. I smiled as he ran towards me. He was a little sweaty from the heavy lifting, and his unbuttoned shirt flapped open with each stride of his long, muscular, legs. Patrick pulled me closer towards him, picked me up, and twirled me around in an incredibly embarrassing display of public affection. Patrick made me feel giddy and treasured, but I was nervous about what the others would think. He slid me down his tall frame until I was eye level with his chest.

That was another thing that had changed since Josiah's kidnapping. Although I've always felt the intense friction of desire between the others and me, our boundaries seem to have become even more blurred over the past few weeks. No matter how much I wanted to convince myself that I've gained a makeshift family in Dormas, there's always the hint of something *more* percolating between us.

"Oh calm down, will you?" Huxley interrupted with a growl. "This isn't date night, you tool. We're going on a fucking mission." He scowled deeply at us while wiping his hands on the denim of his jeans. Jacob rolled his eyes. Huxley's bitter attitude was one thing that hadn't changed.

"You're just pissed you lost," Patrick joked while using the bottom flap of his unbuttoned shirt to wipe the sweat dripping off his chin. I caught a glimpse of his sculpted stomach and released a low, appreciative sigh. Once again, I had to fight the urge to blur the lines of our friendship. With much-controlled effort, I averted my eyes from Patrick's toned body while everyone snickered at his comment.

"Lost what?" I asked, fearing the answer.

Cyler then piped in to answer. "Are you referring to how he lost the vote to bring you along? Or how he lost when we drew straws to decide who gets to sit by you on our hour-long trip? "

Huxley rolled his eyes in response to Cyler's chiding remarks, then slowly made his way towards me. He wore his signature frown, and I noticed the familiar intensity storming in his juniper eyes. Sometimes I thought Huxley and I were making strides in our friendship, but just as I began to grow comfortable towards him, he displayed random bursts of hostility that gave me emotional whiplash.

"Don't look at me like that, Ash," Huxley grumbled with a pained expression that had me questioning why we were still playing this fiery dance with one another. He gave a pointed stare towards Cyler, Jacob, and Patrick, which made them step back to provide us with some privacy.

"We don't need any distractions while we're there. This meeting requires us to tread carefully," he began in a low voice. His eyes refused to meet mine. "Even though I know the Scavengers personally, they're still unpredictable. I don't want another thing to worry about." He ran his hand through his short brown hair, ruffled from the hard work of unloading the cargo off the train. I lingered on the fact that he would worry about me. Huxley cared. No matter how much he aspired to convince me he didn't.

"And he didn't want you to meet his ex-girl-friend," Patrick added with a chuckle which caused Huxley to whirl around and playfully punch him in the side. They both started to wrestle one another, causing large puffs of dirt and sand to kick up and fill the humid air.

I chose to ignore Patrick's statement, as well as the ridiculous yet gnawing fang of envy that demanded to know who she was and how she broke through his armor of arrogance and pride. So *this* is how they got the meeting with the Scavengers.

"Where you guys go, I go," I shouted over them. "We're family, Hux, whether you want to accept it or not. And I don't necessarily want to be cooped up in the house with Jules until you return."

They continued to wrestle. Huxley ignored my statement, and after sitting on Patrick until he cried "MERCY," Huxley went back to work unloading the cargo .

"We'll be fine," Kemper said in a matter of fact tone while scanning through his tablet. "We're meeting with one of the smaller and more civilized tribes. Their chief, Tallis, is fairly progressive. We're hoping that he'll help us get an audience with some of the larger scavenger groups." His clothes were wrinkled, and his hair lacked its usual polished style. I saw the thin outer layer of his cool facade shiver and crack. Regardless of his reassuring words, he was just as anxious about this meeting as the rest of them.

"Now, if we were meeting the Eastern Tribe, we'd need an army. They loot and kill without mercy," Kemper added in an emotionless and bored tone while continuing to click away on his tablet.

Fear clamped down on my heart, and Jacob hit Kemper on the back of the head.

"Way to scare her even more, Kemp!" he griped.

"What?!" Kemper looked back at him in confusion, rubbing his head where Jacob hit him.

"I thought you all didn't get along with the Scavengers, that's why you got Walkers from Galla," I observed.

"We have various delicate alliances with a few of the tribes," Cyler explained while inspecting one of the crates. "But not all of them are willing to agree on peace. Hunger and sickness makes them desperate, and being on the outskirts of the Empire, leaves Dormas vulnerable. Most of our issues are with the East,"

"So why now? Why didn't you try to build an

alliance sooner? Why get Galla involved?" I asked. I wanted to understand Cyler's thoughts and motives.

"We didn't have a bargaining chip before. There is nothing a Scavenger wants more than the Vaccine, and the only way we were going to get that was through an alliance with Galla," Cyler briefly explained.

"What a tangled web," I murmured in response.

After we chatted a bit more, I changed into an outfit more suitable for a formal meeting, and we boarded the train. I looked around the familiar trolley, and it felt like a great ball of burning iron was thudding against my ribs and assaulting my nerves. When I saw the familiar purple trim of the train and a large blood stain on the plush carpet, every instinct within the ventricles of my heart rebelled against being back where I once held tightly to Cyler as he bled out and almost died.

"I feel like us being on this train is a bad omen, Cy," I whispered while the others got comfortable.

"Nonsense, babe. This train is one of my favorite places now."

"Why?" I asked.

"Because this train is where a little Walker stole a bit of this stone heart." He patted his thick chest with an open palm before placing a sketch pad in my lap and closing his eyes for a nap.

The train ride was both too long and too short. Every minute that passed made me feel anxious, and I tapped my pencil against my sketchbook until Cyler grabbed my hand, forcing me to stop fidgeting. His touch had a calming effect on me, and I leaned closer, allowing the strength of his confidence to wash over me in reassuring waves.

The scenery outside changed drastically as the train pushed forward, and soon wild trees obstructed our visibility from every corner. Rogue branches that looked like bony fingers brushed the sides of the train, causing eerie sounds that made my mind conjure up dark scenarios.

"How was your first day at the bakery, Ash?" Kemper asked with a smile.

"It was alright. I fulfilled my first order, but the customer never showed up." I gave Cyler a snide side-eye.

"Because of this meeting, I didn't even get to enjoy it," he grumbled, causing the room to fill with chuckles.

"Come here, I want to show you something," Kemper said while patting the seat next to him. I stepped around the others as they worked on various projects. Once I was seated, Kemp pulled out an intricately carved bear the size of a fist. Each detail was masterfully displayed, and I couldn't stop looking at the beauty of it. Kemper was so skilled.

"Lois mentioned last week that she was going to start selling toys in the shop. I hope you don't mind, but I was the one that told her about your artistic abilities," he said with a wince. Apparently, it was well known how pushy Lois could be.

"Ahh, so *you're* to blame," I replied teasingly.

"Yes, well, I carved this for you. Well, I mean for the kids, but—but for you to paint," he rushed out awkwardly, and I wanted to hug him.

"It's lovely Kemp," I said in awe as he placed it in my hand.

He went over the details of his carving process, and I listened intently, our conversation a welcome distraction from the anxiety that plagued me.

Too soon, the train stopped, and Jacob opened the trolley door, revealing miles and miles of overgrown wilderness. Plush greens and browns filled my vision for as far as I could see, and a robust and earthy scent filled my nose.

"Welcome to the Deadlands," a throaty voice

said. Outside the train, stood a tall, stunning woman. She had long white-blonde hair and deep-brown eyes framed by white lashes. Her nose was narrow, and plump round lips took up a large part of her face. She was wearing black pants, black boots, and a black backless shirt that tied around her neck and exposed a sliver of her stomach. Her eyes brightened when she saw Huxley behind me, and I realized that this ridiculously beautiful woman was Huxley's ex.

Huxley gave me a small and timid glance before gently pushing me aside and making his way down the steps into her outstretched arms. She gracefully wrapped herself around him, and he kissed her on the lips in a brief but intimate display that spoke volumes about their relationship. I clenched my stomach, surprised by the gnawing pain that erupted within me by seeing them together.

"It's so good to see you *Latria Mu* ," she cooed, causing me to choke on the bile that rose up my throat .

"Likewise, Mia," Huxley replied with, dare I say it, *a smile* . Mia got more smiles from Huxley within the first two minutes of their reunion than I've gotten in the entire past month.

"Welcome everyone. My brother is waiting to

speak with you," Mia said with smiling, mischievous eyes. "He's in a particularly good mood, so we must pounce while the opportunity is hot!" she exclaimed in a poised yet cheeky tone. While exiting the train, Mia grabbed my arm and forcefully helped me down the steps. "It's so good to finally meet you. I've heard much about the wild-haired woman that's got my *Latria Mu* all out of sorts." She chuckled while Huxley groaned.

"I'm happy to be here," I politely replied while straightening my ankle-length tawny skirt and cerulean lace top. Mia pulled me closer to her and helped me navigate the wild vines and roots that covered every inch of the forest floor as we made our way towards the Scavenger's tribal center. I eyed the guys, but none of them seemed concerned with the tight, but guiding grip Mia had on me.

"Did any of these men warn you about what to expect today?" she asked in a chiding tone while raising a white eyebrow at me.

"Not really. Everything I know about scavengers, I learned from the Galla news reports, and even those are rare," I replied softly. It felt surreal talking to a Scavenger. Until now they didn't seem human to me.

Mia openly scoffed and snorted, a sound that

somehow made her sound even more attractive. "Galla puts out so much propaganda about my people, they don't know the truth anymore. They don't agree with anything that doesn't conform to the Empire's rules." The bridge of her nose rippled in disgust.

"My brother's name is Tallis. When you meet him, you can address him as such. He's seventeen and officially the youngest Chief to ever pass our leadership trials. He's rough around the edges but don't let him fool you. He's a closet softie," she said with a hint of pride and a smirk. "We might be one of the smaller tribes, but we are wildly protective of what's ours. "

I couldn't help but wonder if she was referring to Huxley.

My eyes widened before snapping to Huxley's back. His rigid figure walked ahead of us, but I noticed his head was tilted towards us as if trying to inconspicuously listen to our conversation.

Mia's chuckle made the dark trees seem less threatening. "Don't worry *Agrio* , he hasn't been mine for quite some time," she whispered. She gave me a knowing glance that said my concern for Huxley was more evident than I intended to let on.

"What does *Agrio* mean?" I asked.

"Simply put, it means Wild one." She smiled, and I noticed that her teeth were unusually sharp, as if she purposefully shaved them into little fine points. I made a mental note to ask Kemper later if that was a common practice amongst Scavengers.

I giggled loudly, causing everyone to direct their attention towards us. Huxley's face turned bright red. "I'm far from wild!" I exclaimed with another giggle. The thought of anyone labeling me as such was beyond humorous, and I belly laughed for the first time in weeks.

"I think you're far wilder than you give yourself credit for, *Agrio* ," Mia replied with a wink.

Before I could respond, a thin man broke through the thick bushes and trees with a moan. Open sores that oozed puss and blood covered his arms and legs. He had sunken eyes and a mysterious appearance that advertised the danger he possessed. He moved like a bundle bones with a faint consciousness controlling them, and wore a frown with rotten teeth that looked like dead flowers in a vacant bed of soil.

An infected Walker.

Before the others could react, Mia grabbed a knife strapped to her thigh and chunked it at his chest. She threw her blade with the practiced speed and precision of a seasoned killer. His hard face softened at the threshold of eternity, and when the walker collapsed on impact, he let out a shrill wheeze that echoed through us. We all stood still as he twitched and groaned until his lifeless body froze, and a sob broke free from my throat.

Maverick trudged up to the lifeless body. He whispered a few words while he poured a foul-smelling brown liquid from a metallic flask over the body. Maverick then nodded his head towards Mia who corralled me away just as he dropped a lit match on the Walker.

"One of the larger neighboring tribes to the West became infected three weeks ago," Mia explained with a shaky voice. The adrenaline from her kill seemed to move with intensity throughout her. "We've had 15 walkers in the past two sun cycles wander near our camp, and two of our own committed suicide after coming into contact with them."

The burning smell invaded my nose even as we walked farther from the body and towards the Scavenger tribal lands. Maverick caught up with us eventually, and I looked towards the sky and watched smoke billow up in puffs. The evidence of what happened coated the air with an ominous hue.

"I extinguished the fire," Maverick told Mia before walking ahead of us and joining Cyler at the head of our group. The Walker's arrival brought a solemn mood, and everyone walked in contemplative silence, each of us mourning the various lives of those the disease claimed.

CHAPTER FOUR

Once we made it towards the center of their camp, I noticed a pattern of bright-orange tarp tents that stood out amongst the abundance of trees. They were strategically placed in a circle, facing a massive white tent in the middle. Campfires roared around us, causing a smoky haze to fill the area. As we arrived, Scavengers emerged from their dwellings and jogged towards us. Children with white hair and mischievous grins ran up to Huxley and embraced him.

It was generally understood that the Deadland's water supply was toxic, causing all the inhabitants to have bleached hair and nails. It also made Scavengers more prone to infection. Still, many preferred the dangerous woods and tainted water supply to the restrictive and segregated nature of the Empire.

"My brother will see us soon, he's meeting with our elders now." Mia gestured for us to sit around a massive blazing fire that burned a strange shade of green.

I found a vacant log to sit on, and Mia plopped down next to me on my left, while Patrick joined me on my right. Patrick gripped my fumbling hand in quiet reassurance, and Mia eyed our entwined fingers with curiosity.

There was a strange and uncomfortable silence between us, and the painfully awkward situation urged me into making polite conversation with Mia.

"How did you and Huxley meet?" I asked, surprising myself with the boldness of the question. I knew that Patrick and Huxley lost their parents to an Eastern Scavenger attack, and it seemed unusual that, despite that, he would become romantically involved with one of them.

"I like to think it was fate that brought Huxley and me together," Mia began while settling in to her seat. "I was on patrol duty, and he was hunting in the Deadlands for food. It was a notably bad harvest year, which made the fool hunt further into the woods than normal. A hog speared him in his right calf with one of his tusks, and I witnessed it. Once he passed out, I placed him on my hover cart and dragged him back here. It took days to mend him. The gash was at least six inches long. Tallis and the elders took bets on how long he'd last.

"After three days, he woke up and immediately started punching the air and cursing all the Scavengers of this God forsaken world—it was all very dramatic." Mia chuckled. "It took some moonshine and a lot of coaxing before I found out that a tribe to the East of us killed his parents." I felt Patrick stiffen beside me at the mention of them.

"I nursed *Latria Mu* back to health. God, in the beginning I thought we were going to kill each other!" Mia exclaimed with a smile. "Each day, he hated me a little bit less until, eventually, he started looking for excuses not to leave. Finally, I just kissed him silly until he admitted that he liked me." She eyed me mischievously.

I looked over at Huxley and felt a deep sadness permeate within me.

"We spent a few months together. It was young, foolish love. We were selfish, but he realized he needed to be home with his brother, and I realized I loved the challenge of him much more than I loved him," Mia said while somehow producing a flask from beneath her skin-tight shirt. She took a swig of its contents with a wince before offering some to me and Patrick. I declined, but Patrick readily accepted. He rolled up his sleeves, revealing his muscular forearms and I watched him as he took a giant gulp and wiped his plump lips with the back of his arm.

"Of course, my brother hates him, so there's also that," Mia exclaimed with a chuckle, pulling me out of my intense observation of Patrick. Dread pooled in the pit of my belly. If her brother hated Huxley, would that mean that he would be unwilling to help us?

The flaps to the large, white tent opened, and an older woman with deep-set wrinkles exited with a solemn expression. Long white hair trailed down her back and frayed at the end.

"The Dormas representatives may join us now," she said in a low tone, causing the entire village to grow silent. We all stood and slowly made our way into the tent.

Once inside, I saw that it was entirely furnished and had a fire pit in the center. More mysterious green flames danced in the center of a pit, and a hole in the ceiling allowed the smoke to clear. The tent comfortably fit twenty people, and on the far wall sat a raised pallet with a wooden chair coated with thick slate furs.

A man with long white hair and green eyes was perched upon it. He was shirtless but wore thick grey pants. Intricate scars in ornate designs covered every visible square inch of his pale skin.

With poised intention, he slowly raised his muscular arm and wordlessly gestured for us to sit. Mia left me and kneeled at his feet, facing us. Cyler sat to my right and Maverick on my left. As if by muscle memory, I tucked my legs beneath my bottom and bowed, a submissive display that Mistress Stonewell forced me to perform whenever she gave me orders or instructions. It was a position I retreated to whenever I felt like I was in a threatening situation.

"Welcome to my home," the man on the makeshift throne covered in furs said. His voice was rich and flowed throughout the tent like warm honey. It contradicted his frightening demeanor.

"Thank you for agreeing to meet with us, Tallis," Cyler's authoritative voice replied. He was usually the one that managed trade negotiations, so I wasn't surprised to see him take charge. He puffed out his chest and stared at Tallis with unyielding strength.

"Of course, my sister has ensured that you'd have

a deal that makes this worth my time. I hope that you don't abuse her faith in you." He slid fierce eyes on Huxley. Huxley returned his glare with equal measure, causing the intensity of the room to increase tenfold.

"We're seeking to build a more beneficial alliance between our communities, "Cyler began. "Although over the past few generations your tribe and my providence have been peaceful towards one another, I think now is the time for our alliance to grow into something more forceful."

I glanced over at Jacob whose chocolate eyes roamed the entire tent, continually checking for any danger or threat.

"I see" was all Tallis said while petting the furs draped over his armrest in a sinister motion.

Cyler remained quiet, and a silent standoff between the two ensued. My eyes pinged between Tallis and Cyler, frantically wondering which alpha leader would react or respond first. It was finally Tallis that broke, which caused a sliver of a smile to creep up on Cyler's face before he masked his joy. Cyler won this little battle.

"And what exactly is to be expected of my people, should we ally together?" Tallis asked.

"Dormas is trying to untangle themselves from

the influence of the Empire. We can no longer sit idly by while they abuse their power, and now we have the resources to succeed."

Cyler's voice rang throughout the tent, and the only sound heard after his declaration was the crackling of the emerald fire. I cautiously looked around, worried that emperorLackley himself was somehow spying on us. To even think of defying the Empire was punishable by death. The fact that Dormas was going as far as to ally with their enemies was terrifying.

"Counting the sins of the Empire doesn't make you a saint, Cyler Black. You watched on the sidelines as my people were pushed deeper into the Deadlands. Besides, you have yet to answer my question," Tallis spit out like his words were venomous.

"I didn't watch from the sidelines. My family and I were struggling to keep Dormas alive. We didn't have the time or the resources to help anyone else," Cyler countered. His knuckles were white from tension.

"What do you want from us? Obviously, you have all the power in this situation. The threat of X is a heavy burden on us," Tallis said with a frown. My thoughts drifted to the infected Walker that blazed through the forest earlier.

"I need your men to fight. I need your connec-
tions with the other tribes; I need your friendship
and your fists." Cyler shrugged as if what he was
suggesting wasn't a huge request.

"You want my men to die for a cause that isn't
theirs," Tallis replied with a snarl. I watched as his
scarred hands gripped the edge of his chair. "We
untangled ourselves from the empire when we fled to
the Deadlands. We struggle through survival enough
as it is, and now you want us to risk more lives for
your people?" The mood of the room plummeted,
and I watched as each participant flexed their
muscles.

"I'm offering you a chance at survival! I'm
offering you the vaccine! You know that whatever
chaos I bring to your doorstep will be worth it. Your
people are dying," Cyler pleaded.

I looked around the room at the others and
wondered if they would jump in to defend Cyler's
deal, but each of them wore silent and brooding
expressions. I thought that the level-headed
Maverick or even the kind Kemper could diffuse the
surmounting situation with Tallis, but it seemed that
each of them was given strict instructions not to
speak. I, however, was not; which is why I packed

away my fear in the darkest parts of my swirling gut and spoke up .

"With all due respect, Tallis," I began, earning various disapproving looks from my guys, and a guttural growl from Huxley. "Your men will die regardless. Influenza X is on your heels. How long do you think it'll be before the Empire is breathing down your necks, too? They take what they want and have a trail of destruction to prove it. Either your men die from X, or they'll die fighting. With us they have more of a chance." I exhaled and stayed motionless, praying I wasn't overstepping or making things worse for Cyler.

"Who are you?" Tallis asked while rising from his throne. He walked around the fire pit and stopped in front of me. My eyes were level with his pale knees until he plopped down and sat cross-legged in front of me. He leaned forward and calmly rested his elbows on his thighs. All authority and seriousness seemed to drain out of him as he openly observed me with the careful gaze of a friend and not the intense glare he wore before.

"I'm... Ash. A newly liberated Walker from the Galla Providence," I answered with mock confidence. My entire body hummed with fluttering assurance. A flustered and annoyed Cyler tried to speak, but Tallis held his gnarled hand up to stop him. He was eerily interested in me.

"I've heard rumors of newly liberated Walkers taking up residence in Dormas. I've often wondered if you were trading one pair of shackles for another. Are you happy there?"

"Yes," I replied without hesitation. My eyes left Tallis' for the briefest of moments to catch an overly pleased grin from Kemper. My admission made him happy.

My eyes flashed back to Tallis. "I was born in the Walker Zones and plucked from my dead mother's arms. I was auctioned off and sold to a prominent family where I was raised to think I was worthless. Dormas is the first taste of freedom I've ever had. It's home."

Tallis looked at me with burning eyes that swept across my face in cool moves. He observed me openly, waiting for a crack in my resolve, so he'd have an excuse to say no .

"Cyler . . . I don't trust. Behind his confidence is greed, I can smell it on him," he said. I immediately opened my mouth to argue with him. Cyler and the guys were the most selfless people I knew, but Tallis continued before I could explain.

"The empire's prejudice unites scavengers and

Walkers alike. Therefore, I trust *you* ." Tallis placed a palm over my heart. The nearness of him made me want to cringe, and I noticed Cyler's fist ball in on itself tightly at Tallis' contact. "We'll migrate to the far east corner of Dormas within the new moon. That will make us close enough to provide protection, but still far enough to be independent. In exchange, we would like vaccines and access to your food supply, as well as paid jobs in the mines." He grabbed my hand, placed it upon his chest, and bowed. I wasn't sure about their customs and was worried that I sealed the agreement somehow.

Cyler then interrupted with a grin and immediately jumped in on making plans. "Yes, of course. Your terms are acceptable. We will include your community in our rationing schedule, and there is more than enough work in the mines. What about the other tribes, will you help us build alliances?" The hope that dripped off of Cyler's tone was all-encompassing, he seemed over-eager and anxious for Tallis' cooperativeness.

Once again, Tallis didn't address Cyler and kept his eyes on me. Somehow, in saying that I was a Walker, my authority over this meeting surpassed Cyler's. I shivered under Tallis' intense stare, and Maverick placed his hand on my lower back, giving me the strength to stay still and not flee the tent. I noticed Tallis' eyes linger on Maverick for a brief moment before flickering back to me.

"We will send runners to neighboring tribes that have formed an alliance with us and schedule a council meeting after the month's end. I cannot guarantee that they will listen, let alone attend, but I will try."

I nodded and smiled timidly at Tallis while Mia whistled loudly, disrupting the severe mood of the tent. "A deal made without bloodshed! My little *Agrio* is good luck! "

I smiled at Mia and quickly understood what Huxley saw in her. Mia's good nature was infectious. A sliver of a smile graced Tallis' face, and I saw a glimpse of the man beneath the authoritative facade. When he wasn't scowling or wearing the burden of his people on his back, he almost looked like the young man he was. The stress and burden of his people's safekeeping aged him considerably. I realized that he and the Dormas Leadership Council had a kinship of sorts. They were all men forced to grow up quickly.

After a solidifying a few more details between Cyler and Tallis, we made our way back to the train. Now that the seriousness of the meeting was over,

Tallis completely abandoned all formalities and accompanied us back. It was well past midnight by then, and the moon illuminated the woods in a shimmery yet unnatural glow, hinting that something abnormal was lingering within the elemental makeup of the trees.

"I think *Agrio* is a good nickname for our new friend, Mia. Even her hair is wild." He chuckled in a friendly manner and pinched one of my curls between his fingers. He had slowed down to walk with me back to the train. Huxley remained close and scowled at Tallis whenever he got the chance, making it clear that despite their new alliance, he still didn't necessarily like him. I yearned to explore the history between them and hoped I got the opportunity to ask Mia when she moved closer to Dormas.

"I've never been able to tame it," I replied with a self-deprecating chuckle.

Tallis' sharp teeth flashed in the dark before he spoke, "Tame nothing about yourself, *Agrio* ," he whispered seriously. That earned him a literal growl from Huxley who wrapped his thick hand around my own.

Tallis sent Huxley a knowing grin. "It's nice to see that you've moved on from my sister." He then whistled playfully to himself and walked ahead of us to speak with Kemper.

As Tallis walked away, Huxley stuttered out in delayed response, "I—I don't know what you're talking about." This caused both Mia and Tallis to break out in booming laughter that ricocheted off the glowing trees and vines.

Once on the train, we said our goodbyes and unloaded crates of the vaccine. I smiled, thinking about all the Scavenger children that would receive it. Mia wrapped me in a long hug that left me feeling confused about everything I thought I knew about the Scavengers and their way of life.

These people were kind. They were eccentric but still pleasant. She also wrapped Huxley in a friendly hug, and I saw the history between them, but also saw that their relationship was purely platonic, despite it. I left the Deadlands seeing the Scavengers as a little more human and, once again, questioned the humanity of the Galla leaders.

CHAPTER FIVE

I fell asleep on Kemper's shoulder during the ride back home. The adrenaline and anxiety left me feeling exhausted. However, I was disappointed that I didn't soak up as much time as possible with the guys before we were back in Dormas and under Jules' determined reign. When I woke up to Kemper's sweet smile and tentative hand on my arm, I almost forgot all the troubles that plagued us.

"You did great last night," he whispered while lifting me up in his arms and carrying me outside the train. The sun had just started to rise, and Cyler had the transport ready to take me back to the manor, so we wouldn't have to walk in our exhausted state. Kemper carefully placed me in the leather bucket seat next to Cyler, and I was amazed by his strength and control despite his smaller frame.

Jacob sadly waved goodbye while making his way to his office at the train station, and concern enveloped me. I hated that he didn't feel like he could come home. I made a mental note to corner him and discuss it later. The house felt empty without Jacob's flirtatious presence, and I wanted us to go back to the way things were before she reclaimed her toxic place in their lives. Something needed to happen with Jules' living arrangements and soon .

"I feel like I haven't slept in days," I said in a tired voice while snuggling deeper into Cyler's muscular side. I used my sleepy state as an excuse to be close to him. Kemper leaned inside the open transport door, and I noticed that he, too, seemed exhausted and worn down.

"Come on, babe, let's go home," Cyler said in a soothing tone while rubbing small circles on my lower back. We made our way back and quietly entered the manor. All of us were careful not to make any noise and alert Jules of our presence.

Most nights, I slept in Jacob's now vacant room, but Cyler wordlessly guided me towards his room. I was too tired to fight him over the sleeping arrangements. Not to mention, a small part of me reveled in the idea of falling into the security and comfort Cyler offered. I still struggled with the confusing dynamic between us.

We bypassed all awkwardness and slid fully clothed beneath the white covers of his bed. I forced myself not to examine what this meant or worry about what the others would think. We simply fell into a deep sleep.

***

"How very *interesting* ."

A high-pitched voice rang throughout my dreams, causing my eyes to flutter open and observe my surroundings. I was nestled into a hot chest, and a broad hand was tightly clutching the curve of my butt, pulling me close to a solid frame. Light snores filled the space around me, and after a few blinks, I remembered where I was and who I was with. I tried squirming out of Cyler's hold, but he merely clutched me tighter, causing a wave of tingles to shoot to my core.

"Ah, babe, keep still, you're so warm," Cyler whispered in a breathy voice. A cruel laugh reminded me that we weren't alone, and Cyler woke with a start. Once shaking the sleep from his eyes, he immediately withdrew himself from me, sat up, and piled the thick, cotton comforter on his lap .

Somehow in the middle of the night he lost his shirt, and I couldn't help but stare at his defined chest and abs. I drank in his big-shouldered tapering silhouette and bit my bottom lip. His eyes shifted to me, and he sighed in frustration before grabbing my chin and rotating my head so that my gaze was away from him and on our intruder. Jules leaned against the door frame with a smug smile on her face. She peered at us with a strategic coldness.

"I guess your all night picnic with Jacob ended in Cyler's bed," she sneered while looking me up and down. "How devastatingly *scandalous*!"

I still wore my outfit from the day before. The thin blue straps became loose and stretched in my sleep, causing one to slide off my shoulder, revealing my generous cleavage. We looked downright disgraceful, despite our formerly innocent intentions. I briefly thought of Cyler's sleepy yet hard grasp on my butt, and the heat of embarrassment filled me.

"Get OUT!" Cyler ordered while throwing a pillow at her. Jules laughed as she walked away while humming to herself. I turned to face Cyler, but he avoided my gaze.

"We've got to do something about her. I'm making her new home a priority on Kemper's building list!" His yelling caused me to flinch. I scooted closer to him and bravely wrapped my arms around his waist. Anger spilled through him like a stain, and I desperately tried to fix the defect that was Jules Black.

I rested my chin on his shoulder and felt him relax under my hold. A small part of me liked that I could relax him. It gave me a sense of power I've never felt before. Eventually, the anger fled his body, and he began to sit without the hold of fury and a monotonous craving formed between us.

"Ignore her, that's what I do," I mumbled in a gentle tone while breathing in his scent. The hint of smoke stuck to his clothes, reminding me of the infected walker. I pulled away and peered into Cyler's eyes.

"Did you sleep well?" I asked while scrutinizing his appearance .

"Better than I've slept in years, babe." The reply was followed by a cheeky grin and knowing look. His long hair was crimped and frizzy, showing evidence of his excellent sleep.

"I slept well, too. You make me feel safe, Cy," I said truthfully, while shifting the blankets over my chest. Cyler eyed me and lifted a hand to adjust the strap of my dress. With tentative fingers, he pulled it higher up on my shoulders. His large hands lingered near my collarbone, lightly stroking the frame of my neck and causing a series of fireworks to erupt and shatter my senses.

"You can't say things like that to a man, babe."

"Why not?" I asked, although already feeling the hidden meaning of his words. Once again, I was dancing between the line of what was right and what I wanted.

"Because he just might fall in love with you." His voice was hoarse and spoke volumes about the intensity of this moment. I felt like Cyler and I were standing on the edge of the cliff, and both of us were daring the other to jump; to admit that there was more between us than friendliness.

However, neither of us leaped and said what we wanted to. We separately got ready for the day, then made our way downstairs in time for a late snack. Awkwardness hung between us like a heavy fog.

After sleeping most of the day away, I felt refreshed despite Jules' intrusion. Downstairs, Kemper was typing away at the kitchen table, and

Cyler immediately began discussing with him plans to relocate Jules into a new home—on the complete opposite side of the providence.

Maverick was cooking omelets and taking our orders when my tablet rang throughout the room, causing everyone to halt what they were doing immediately.

The only person that called me was Josiah, and we hadn't spoken since I was abducted and used as a pawn in the Emperor's games. Everyone stilled and stared at me, eager to see what I would do. An inner conflict made me pause. Josiah was my oldest friend, but his betrayal still stung .

The guys intently watched as I glided over to my tablet and answered the video call. In another time, I might have excused myself and relished in the privacy and comfort of Josiah, but I didn't feel those familiar flutters of lust or even familiarity. I didn't know him, not really.

Besides, even from across the tablet, fear spread through me like a vibrating tone, reminding me of how he clutched me and kissed me without permission. Or how he drugged me and used me in the cruel practices of the Empire.

When the screen came to life, and I saw Josiah sitting in the dark of the basement, I wanted to feel sorry for him. I wanted those delicate whispers of love to unfold upon me, to remind me that it was us—always us. But they never came. He looked disheveled and broken, and my heart felt nothing.

"Hey, Ash," he choked out in a whisper.

"Hey." Looking at the dimly lit basement made my stomach churn. It was hard to think that a few short weeks ago, that was my home.

"I have to be careful now when I call you. We can't talk for long, but I needed to see the birthday girl." A small smile graced his peach lips, and I let loose the hint of a grin. Even though my heart was hardening, our friendship and care somewhat remained. Josiah always found a way to make me feel special on my birthday. As a young boy, he would sneak chocolates and other knick-knacks wrapped in newspaper into my room so I would have a gift to open.

I checked the date on my tablet and was surprised to see that today was, in fact, my birthday. I then glanced up and saw Cyler glaring at me with eyes meaner than a bee sting. I briefly worried that he was upset that Josiah called.

"You forgot again, didn't you?" Josiah joked, but the smile didn't quite reach his eyes.

"You know I don't usually celebrate." My eyes

glided back down to the tablet, ignoring the angry stares from Cyler, Maverick, and Kemper .

"The day you were born is a day that the entire Empire should celebrate, Ashleigh."

I smiled and was pleased by his words, but once again my emotions felt hollow. There was a time that I might have swooned at his admission, but not anymore. If anything, I was embarrassed by his flirtatious comment, and it made me blush. A cough reminded me that we had an audience, and I kept my expressions under control. Despite all the time, pain, and distance, Josiah still managed to fluster me.

"Normally, I would have a gift for you, but this year I'm just going to have to trust that Cyler or one of your...friends...will take care of it." He spoke loudly as if knowing that someone was listening in on our conversation.

"Remember the one birthday when we went dancing in the courtyard?" he asked in a hopeful tone that didn't match his dark and brooding appearance.

I did. Josiah stole a merlot chiffon dress from his mother's closet, and I clumsily wore it. It was way too big and slipped off my slender shoulders, but I still remembered how Josiah's eyes swept appreciatively over me. We snuck out at midnight and danced until our feet hurt.

His keen eyes had roamed my body, his hands lingering upon my hips while we danced. It was one of the first nights that I wondered if his feelings mimicked mine. I wondered if he desired me as much as I desired him.

I slowly nodded while puffing air out, pushing a curl that had fallen in my eyes. I was unwilling to answer Josiah's question for fear that everyone would hear the crack of emotion in my voice. It was one of the few memories I had of Josiah before everything went to hell. Before he got engaged. Before he chose his duties over me. Before I got swept away into the Dormas providence with my new family.

"I hope one day we can dance together again," he whispered while looking longingly at me.

"Just tell me what's going on, Josiah. I can help you. We can help you." I wanted desperately to understand what was going on. Some twisted part of me still wanted a happy ending for Josiah. I wanted —no, needed to know that he would be okay, despite all this pain between us.

"You can help me by staying as far away from Galla and emperorLackley as possible. You have no idea what's brewing." I noticed his temple angrily throb.

"Then *tell me,*" I pleaded once more.

"Stay safe, Ash. I love you." And with that, the line clicked, leaving an empty screen and my empty heart.

I wasn't sure how to feel at Josiah's sudden departure. Sometimes I think he reveled in having the last laugh or leaving me to wonder. I once would agonize over every word he spoke to me and replay in my mind over and over every inflection of his golden tone. But instead, I felt a new feeling at his departure —relief.

Cyler was itching to say something, and the moment I lifted my eyes to his, it was like a dam breaking.

"I can see here that you're dealing with some major internal turmoil, but I'd like to pause briefly on this heartbreak to scold you for not telling us that your birthday is TODAY!" Cyler yelled, and the room reverberated with his anger. Maverick and Kemper wore equal looks of disapproval.

"I forgot!" I exclaimed with a shaky voice, still distraught from my conversation with Josiah, and the lack of emotions I felt when seeing his face. My words snapped Maverick into action as he used his

tablet to call everyone and let them know that a celebration was in order. He worked with the efficiency
of a true leader as he dialed numbers and barked
orders.

"Who do we call to bake a cake when it's the
baker's birthday?" Kemper mused. His usual kind
smile was playful as he looked me over. He didn't
seem nearly as worried and stressed as the others.

"Jacob's got guard duty tonight, but I can make
arrangements for someone else to keep an eye out on
our prisoners for the night," Cyler said .

Josiah's Galla guards were held in a warehouse
turned jail on the outskirts of town. Each of the guys,
and a few trusted Dormas citizens, took turns
patrolling the grounds to make sure they didn't
escape. Even though the disease Maverick infected
them with caused them to pass out whenever their
heart rate increased, they were still a formidable
threat.

"Jacob doesn't need to give up his shift. We don't
have to celebrate!" I urged.

"Oh gosh, I thought we passed the martyr stage,
Cy. Guess we need to remind our girl how special
she is." Maverick smirked while grazing over the
term 'our girl.'

I quietly stood there while they frantically ran

around making plans for an impromptu birthday party.

How did I go from forgetting today was my birthday one moment, to a full-blown celebration the next?

CHAPTER SIX

I somehow managed to convince Cyler that the entire town didn't need to be invited over to celebrate. He originally wanted a party comparable to the Summer Solstice, but I immediately vetoed that. Still, everyone moved with frantic energy while preparing dinner and dessert for me. I ignored the rushed and whispered calls to some of the local shops as they tried to coordinate, and giggled when Lois scolded them for not planning ahead, until of course, she started scolding me for not telling her about my birthday.

As if attracted to the commotion, Jules positioned herself at the kitchen table and threw out undiluted scorn to anyone within earshot. Her beautiful face twisted into a look of disapproval, and her indignant huffs increased the temperature with each of her scornful remarks.

"I don't understand why everyone is making such a big deal about this. Even the Walker didn't remember her own birthday." Jules snorted, apparently finding herself hilarious. "On my birthday, Jacob was the only one that called."

"That's because on your birthday, while you were safe and sound at school, *we* were dealing with an attack from the Eastern Scavengers," Maverick said.

"I could have been home helping you all, but then you'd just complain that I was in the way," Jules countered.

"That's because you *would* have been in the way," Maverick replied. She crossed her thin arms over her chest in annoyance.

"Oh, Jules!" Cyler said with a half-smile while whirling around to face her. His large, calloused fingers were struggling to tie small scraps of string together to make decorative multi-colored streamers. "I'm so glad you're here. I've been meaning to talk to you. I didn't get the opportunity to chat this morning because, as you're well aware, I was indisposed." My cheeks blushed at the reminder of this morning and Cyler's large, perfect hands on me.

Maverick stopped chopping fruit and exchanged a small but pleased smile with Cyler before crossing his arms and angling his body towards Jules, demonstrating a united front between the two of them. I briefly wondered if their family dynamic was usually like this, the two brothers ganging up on their younger sister.

"Since the engagement with Josiah is permanently broken off, I think we need to revisit the terms of your punishment. We gave you a few weeks to settle back into Dormas, but now we must move forward with your disciplinary terms." The smirk on Jules' face promptly disappeared, and I noticed an echo of fear reflected in her eyes before she slipped into her signature stoic poker face.

"It's not my fault the engagement is off. That Josiah guy was a *total* buzzkill. He didn't even try. He just moped in his room and played on his tablet. Then the emperorcame over, and within the hour we were in a transport headed for here."

I noticed the guys exchange varying looks of concern before bringing their attention back to her. She just confirmed what we already knew; the emperor was behind Josiah's impromptu visit. I wanted to ask her more about Lackley's intentions but allowed Maverick and Cyler to handle it. But I was more than curious. What hold did Lackley have over Josiah ?

Jacob's abrupt cough shook me out of my thoughts. His hair was wet as if he just showered, and he wore a form-fitting, button-down shirt tucked into grey slacks that showed off his muscular legs. Our eyes connected, and he smiled before glancing at Jules and walking upstairs. His movements were controlled and stiff with tension.

"To speak plainly, we were all *exceedingly* disappointed to hear that things didn't work out with Josiah," Maverick interrupted with an eye roll. "I know you were excited by the prospect of becoming a Governor's wife; however, since you're back on Dormas lands we've decided that you are to work in the gardens with some of the new Walkers. We all pull our weight around here, and for too long we've allowed you to get by without contributing. You've never really had a job. Plus, I think it's time you move out of the manor. This home is for the Dormas leadership council." Maverick's face was fierce and unyielding. "Kemper kindly prepared a temporary room for you in the Walker Dorms, and you will be put on the waitlist for a cabin, contingent upon you working well with the other Walkers."

Jules' face bloomed a bright red, and her cruel

eyes looked me over as if I held the secrets to her banishment and that it was *my* fault that this was happening to her. I flinched under her scrutiny, and Kemper moved behind me while placing a gentle hand on my waist. His support anchored me, and I was immediately comforted by his presence.

"If this house is for leadership council members only, then why is *she* here?" she snarled.

"Because she manages our home," Cyler shrugged, and a slight stabbing pain poked me in the heart. Was that honestly the only reason they kept me around?

"More like she's the house whore!" Jules barked in frustration, and Kemper gripped me harder against him. I wasn't sure if he was trying to hold me back from saying anything or if he was holding himself back. I wanted to defend myself but knew it was pointless. Jules was ruthless and stuck in her ways. She couldn't be reasoned with, and anything I said would be useless .

Huxley, who had been quietly observing our exchange, took menacing strides up to her until his tall frame was standing over her. In a voice so low that I had to strain to hear, Huxley said through clenched teeth, "You better watch your words, Jules. The gardens were a mild punishment compared to what I had planned for you in the mines. Leave within the hour. You're no longer welcome here. You haven't been for a while now."

A small stream of tears began gracefully falling down her angled cheeks, and she peered at Cyler and Maverick with such hurt that I felt an inexplicable urge to defend her, but I bit my lip, knowing that she had a history of lying and being manipulative.

"You both have pushed me away since Mother and Father died. I've spent my entire life hoping you'd one day include me in your little gang, but you never let me in." She gestured to the guys that stood awkwardly around the room. None of them willing to meet her gaze. "One day, you'll have to stop coming up with excuses for why you don't want me around." She puffed out her lower lip then licked up a stray tear. "Besides, your little Walker Whore will go crawling back to Josiah one way or another."

With a huff, Jules straightened her spine, and all sincerity and softness fled her body. She ran to her room where we heard the slamming of doors and drawers. A small crash caused me to flinch. She was apparently trashing the place.

Once she was out of earshot, everyone exhaled, and Jacob rounded the corner, headed towards me.

He pulled me away from Kemper and embraced me in a hug that border-lined on the gray area between friendship and something more. I coughed uncomfortably, still feeling unsure how to act around them all.

"I'm sorry you had to go through that," Jacob whispered. I wanted to reply. I wanted to reassure him and make him feel confident, but words escaped me. How could I make him see what was so plainly in front of him? They chose *him.*

"Let the party begin!" Patrick shouted while clapping his hands loudly. The tension was too much, and as usual, he was trying to diffuse the ominous fog that had settled over us. The sudden shift caused Jacob to extract himself from me and a strange chill took his place. I liked hugging him, all of them, way more than I should.

Jacob moved over to the corner of the kitchen and leaned against the wall. He felt separate from us, and I wanted to make him feel included again. His eyes were downcast, and I assumed that he was once again questioning how they were handling the Jules situation and if there was something he could have done differently.

Maverick opened the oven, and a spicy scent filled the air, which made my mouth water. "I made a traditional Ethros dish; I hope you don't mind. We just started a trade agreement with them," he explained. Ethros was a hot southern Providence with spicy foods and temperamental people. Josiah frequently told me about his brief adventures there.

"Smells delicious. I could get used to someone else doing all the cooking," I joked, trying to follow Patrick's lead and lighten the mood. Maverick's eyes snapped to mine.

"Oh dang. I didn't think this through at all." He scratched his neck. "I should have made something disgusting, so I wouldn't have to cook ever again." He threw a look of terror towards the others, causing loud laughter to echo throughout the room.

"You and I both know that I won't let anyone else do the cooking. Especially since I'm here to simply '*manage the household,* '" I scolded, hoping that someone would provide a sliver of reassurance that me being hired help wasn't the only reason the guys let me stay around.

"Does our little Ash need to hear how much we appreciate her?" Patrick cooed while walking over and ruffling my hair. He then sat down at the large kitchen table and leaned back in the wooden chair while scooting his hips forward. I watched his shirt ride up and swallowed.

"Would you feel better if I gave you a spot on the leadership council? What's a good title you could have?" Cyler mused. He had resumed tying the strings together to make a streamer, but it looked more like a tangled mass of yarn.

"Chief Officer of Chocolate Cakes?" Kemper suggested while icing his own sad attempt at dessert. Uncooked batter oozed over the sides of the pan and mixed with the watery icing. My fingers itched to take over.

"How about Captain of Walker Relations?" Maverick offered. He seemed to take Cyler's suggestion seriously as he sprinkled shredded cheese over the top of his dish in meticulous and equal proportions. I half expected him to get out a ruler to make sure there was no section of the dinner with more cheese than another.

"I don't need a spot on the leadership council. I just need . . ." I paused searching for the words that accompanied my feelings. When I first moved to Dormas, I was content being hired help. I reveled in it. But now? Now I wanted to know that I meant more to them. "I need to feel like you *like* having me here."

Everyone immediately stopped what they were doing to stare at me. The earlier playfulness seemed to dissolve into my ridiculous statement, and I wanted nothing more than to travel back in time and swallow my words.

"JULES!!" Cyler bellowed causing my eyes to widen. I felt a growing panic of self-consciousness consume me. Soon, high heels clacked angrily across the wooden floor until Jules entered the kitchen. She was still scowling, and her hair was all out of place. She looked wild. Feral.

"What the hell do you want now?!" she asked while clutching a broken lamp.

"I just wanted to add, in case there is any confusion, Ashleigh is allowed to stay here 'cause we *like* her." He waved his muscular arm nonchalantly. "That is all."

Jules puffed out her chest and shrilled, "ASS-HOLE!" while walking away. I openly gaped at Cyler. Was that seriously necessary ?

"Better, babe?" he asked with a smirk. I shook my head and slumped in embarrassment. They were always pushing me to vocalize my wants and needs. In his own weird way, Cyler was rewarding me for saying what I wanted. I just wished I would have thought before speaking.

An unalterable promise hovered in the air. One that showed how tightly knit we had become. For the past month, I've felt like I was lingering on the line of uncertainty with Jules' presence. Cyler's unwavering decision regarding Jules' place here and her punishment not only solidified Jacob's position, but mine, too. For the first time since my abduction, I didn't feel like I had to hide.

Dinner was a pleasant affair. The Ethros dish Maverick prepared was heavenly, and I was politely urged by Jacob to stop moaning after every bite. Apparently, I had a bad habit of making too much noise when good food was involved. We all declined dessert, despite a hopeful Kemper and the saddest looking cake I've ever seen. He looked at me in dawning dismay, and I briefly wondered if Kemper was ever bad at anything or if this was his first failure.

Patrick clapped his hands, "It's time for presents!" he said while shuffling in through the kitchen door with a grin. He pulled out a small wooden box. "I'd like to add that finding thoughtful gifts last minute is damn near impossible; you're lucky the people of this Providence love us." He handed me the gift. I peered around the table and saw that each of them wore various looks of uncertainty, nervousness, and eagerness.

For reasons unknown to me, my reaction to this

gift was important to them. I never had the full attention of a room before, and my skin felt hot under their intense stares. The wooden box opened, and I sucked in a deep breath, amazed at the beautiful treasure tucked inside.

It was a golden bracelet wrapped in six different colored raw gems with an inscription on the inside .

Σπίτι μου είναι όπου είμαι μαζί σου

"It's beautiful, what does it mean?" I asked in a shaky voice. This gift was not only thoughtful, but incredibly intimate.

"'Home is wherever you are,'" Jacob answered in a smoky voice. The truth of his statement hit me like a rock, and a silent tear rolled down my cheek. I've never felt more at home than here in Dormas. Here with them.

"It's in the Dormas native tongue. Our parents spoke it," Maverick added matter-of-factly.

"They loved to use it when talking about something they didn't want us to hear," Patrick added with a snicker.

"There are only a handful of Elders left that speak it now. Lois is the one that translated it for us," Maverick added in a sad tone. Once again, I was reminded of all Dormas had lost, and the sincerity of their gift deepened. They were once again inviting me into their past and allowing me to bury myself deep in life here in Dormas. I wiped away an escaped tear and looked around the room. How did I get so lucky?

"I picked the gems," Huxley added with a gruff voice that masked his emotion. I looked down at my bracelet wrapped in navy blue, coral, and black stones, and I saw the sincerity of his choices. Each color represented a part of me and a part of my life here.

The bracelet was quite possibly the most thoughtful and kindest gift I've ever received. I wondered how the guys could have coordinated such a beautiful treasure in such a short amount of time. I immediately slipped it onto my wrist then sprang from my seat, eager to hug everyone. Huxley was closest, and I slammed into him with so much force that he almost fell over.

"Don't kill me over a bracelet." He coughed while fighting a smile. He glared at the others, daring them to comment on our embrace, but I ignored his failed attempt to seem uncaring.

"Thank you," I whispered while nuzzling into him. With exploratory arms, he hugged me back, and his hands drifted to my lower back. I felt such peace and contentment in his embrace. Despite his reluctance, I knew that he had grown to care for me. He lightly lingered until finally pushing me away with a frown and a shake of his head. The moment was gone, and I wondered when he would allow himself to break down his barriers again.

The rest of them took their turns hugging me and inspecting the bracelet upon my wrist. I loved the feel of each of them holding my hand; some scrutinized for much longer than necessary, as if prolonging our contact. But none of them lingered quite like Huxley did. He was acting curious, and I wondered what his sudden transformation meant.

Was I no longer a threat? Or was there something else brewing between us? Between all of us. Something that I wasn't ready to admit to myself, let alone to all of them.

I tried to clean up the mess they made in the kitchen, but I was ushered out and scolded by Patrick. We gathered in the backyard where Kemper had set up a fire pit surrounded by some of his handcrafted wooden chairs. The atmosphere briefly reminded me of the Summer Solstice celebration but this was much quainter and less intense. I settled into a chair around the pit, and Patrick turned on some music with a soft guitar and light beat.

"I've saved the day!" Cyler exclaimed while

walking out with a platter full of strawberries. "Since you didn't get your birthday cake," he continued while rolling his eyes at an embarrassed Kemper. "I know how much you love strawberries, and I grabbed some from Lois."

I remembered the last time I ate strawberries, and how Cyler's confident fingers placed a juicy one covered in chocolate on my tongue. A part of me wished that he would hand feed me again. Would he lick the juices from the corner of my mouth?

I threw my hand over my chest at those fleeting thoughts and widened my eyes in embarrassment. Cyler peered at me with knowing eyes, as if he, too, was remembering our time in the Stonewell kitchen and how intense things already were between us. He kneeled at my side and handed me a plate.

After waiting until everyone was distracted with one of Jacob's long-winded stories, he leaned in close and whispered in my ear, "Would you like for me to feed you again, babe?" I gulped, causing Cyler to grin and bite his lip.

Feeling pleased with my reaction to him, Cyler left the plate and went back to the others. Kemper walked behind me and began massaging my shoulders while I slowly indulged in the strawberries.

"I'm sorry I ruined your cake, Ash. I promise I'll

make it up to you," Kemper said with a sigh. I realized he was more upset than he previously let on.

"Kemper, nothing about tonight is ruined. Tonight is perfect," I said as his nimble fingers worked the knots on my shoulders. I reached up and grabbed his hand, then slightly squeezed. Kemper froze at my touch, and I felt his earlier anxiety disappear under our contact. I couldn't remember a time that I was so treasured and pampered.

Everyone joked, and I observed them openly. I watched how they interacted with one another and how they wholly accepted me into their group. It was jarring to consider who I was just months ago and who I am now. It was in that moment that decided I would do whatever it took to keep my new life here in the Dormas Providence. Here with these kind and thoughtful men that chiseled their way into my heart.

CHAPTER SEVEN

M y bedroom was utterly ruined thanks to Jules' destructive departure. Stained and torn bed sheets covered the mattress. The beautiful windows were covered and smudged with makeup and marks made from coal. Shattered glass littered the floor, and a few of my belongings were ripped and shredded. All my clothes were missing, aside from a few paint-splattered dresses.

Cyler cursed when he saw the mess, but with a swipe of his tablet he bought me an entirely new wardrobe from the most exquisite shop in Galla. I asked him about new bedding, but he slyly insisted that I could just use one of their beds, and he would order bedding another day.

After a chorus of playful arguing and a few arm

wrestling contests, I ended up sleeping in Patrick's bed. Unlike the night before with Cyler, I felt embarrassed and nervous to sleep near Patrick. When he slipped off the thin material of his t-shirt and let it fall to the floor, I practically melted.

His green eyes had a playful sparkle in them as he looked at me from the bathroom, where he was brushing his teeth. He ran a handful of water through his short brown hair, and droplets trickled down his face. Once he was done, he made his way over to me and slipped under the frost-colored covers after turning off the lamplight. I sent up a whisper of thanks for the dark which concealed my blush and the look of longing on my face.

"Did you have a good birthday, Ash?" Patrick whispered into the darkness as I turned away from him. The electric tension between us charged the air with static making it feel heavy.

"It was perfect. It was my first true birthday party, aside from my mini rendezvous with Josiah."

Patrick stilled, and only the sounds of his deep breaths could be heard throughout his room. I instantly regretted mentioning Josiah. I was always ruining these moments.

"It's okay to talk about him," he ambivalently assured. "I'm actually thankful for the bastard. He might be a deranged, bratty psycho, but he showed you kindness in Galla. Without him, I might not have had the chance to meet you." It was dark throughout the room, but I imagined Patrick forcing a smile. He was always the one trying to make me feel better. Patrick perpetually looked for the positive in a situation.

"Thank you for my bracelet," I whispered, feeling desperate to change the subject.

"It was Huxley's idea, you know." I sensed that there was more he wanted to say as he shifted to get comfortable. "Don't hurt him, Ash," Patrick finally said.

"What do you mean?"

"I mean," he began slowly, "I've never seen him like this. I've never seen him fight so hard against something. I've never seen him be thoughtful or *happy* , even," Patrick rushed out, and I wondered if we were talking about the same person.

"Huxley is–" I began.

"Huxley is challenging. He's moody and a pain in the ass. All my life, I just wanted him to be happy. I'd give him anything, except . . .," Patrick trailed off.

"Except what?" I prodded .

"Except lately I'm feeling particularly selfish, which means I'm going to have to leave it up to you to not do the hurting, because at this point, it's inevitable that I'm going to," Patrick replied cryptically.

I wondered about Patrick and Huxley's relationship and how draining it must be to feel so responsible for one another. That sort of anguish and misguided intent was a breeding ground for resentment. I just didn't know how to fix it for them, or even if I could. I was already struggling with my attraction to each of the guys. If what Patrick said was true, that Hux had *changed* since meeting me, was I going to put a deeper wedge between them?

"Lately I just feel so wrong, Patrick," I said. Patrick's firm hand landed on my shoulder and gently pulled me until we were facing one another. His hot minty breath hit my face, and every nerve ending in my body went wild with sensitivity. The cold sheets on his bed suddenly felt heavy, and I squirmed under the weight of his proximity.

"What feels wrong, Ash?" he asked quietly, and I heard the hint of a tremor in his voice. I didn't want them to think it was *them* that was wrong. It was me. My wants. My conflicting thoughts. My desires.

"When I first arrived in Dormas, I was so in love with Josiah. My feelings for him eclipsed everything," I began while briefly remembering the lovesick Walker from Galla with disdain. "But now, I'm not sure. I'm feeling conflicted. I still have affection for Josiah—he's been in my life for as long as I can remember—but for the first time, I love myself more." My words felt rushed and heavy on my tongue. "And I know I'm supposed to be like a sister to you all, but I'm struggling to make my heart commit to that sort of relationship. This doesn't *feel* sisterly. I can't stand feeling like I'm going to ruin everything." Admitting the troubled thoughts that had plagued me made my voice shake at the truth of them.

There was a time that I thought loving someone from afar would be enough. I was comfortable knowing that I would never be good enough for Josiah. It was a mentality ingrained in me by my birthright. I took every last scrap of happiness thrown my way and was thankful for it.

But now? I wanted it all. I wanted to claim my life for my own. I didn't want to settle for lingering looks in the hallway or secretive touches that left me wanting more. I craved blatant love. I wanted to feel treasured.

Patrick remained quiet but snaked his hand around my hips. His feather-light fingertips slipped under my cotton shirt so that his heated touch caressed my bare skin.

"I think we all gave up on viewing you as a sister a while ago," Patrick began. His leg surged forward and tangled between mine. "Does this feel wrong, Ashleigh?" His voice was a husky whisper.

I gulped.

"N—no," I replied.

He then inched closer to me and forced our foreheads to touch. The ghost of his eyelashes danced across mine. "How about this?"

Yes, I thought. "No," I whispered. My voice shook with tension. Patrick was so close yet so far. He then moved so that his lips lingered on mine. I could feel each breath he took.

"Does this feel wrong to you, Ashleigh?" he asked slowly, and I felt each word move against my lips in a seductive dance. I ached to lean closer, to close the last millimeter between us, to feel his lips on mine. I felt tension worming sharp little fingers under my skin and pooling in the bottom of my stomach.

"No," I replied, my voice barely audible. Patrick pulled back in an achingly slow manner, as if each inch between us caused him pain. Despite the distance, he still kept his hand firmly on my hip.

"Don't confuse *wrong* with *unsure* , Ash," he said in a tense voice. "We've been fighting this since the moment you slammed open those train doors and turned our world upside down." He placed his other hand against my collarbone, and his fingers gently curled around my shoulder. It was a slightly possessive gesture that made my heart increase in tempo.

"I'm going to fix this, I promise you. You should never feel guilty for what you want. We want you to have freedom in *all* things. This . . .," Patrick began while pointing his finger and gesturing between us, "changed when Josiah abducted you. I don't think anyone is willing to give you up now, and I promise you that this isn't one-sided."

A loud knock shocked the two of us out of our intimate embrace, and we frantically worked to detangle ourselves. But, we didn't move fast enough to prevent our intruder from seeing our nearness and my flushed face.

Light flooded Patrick's room, and I glanced up to see a very distraught Maverick in the doorway. His dark eyes briefly grazed over my dazed appearance and ruffled clothes. I noted the hint of a wince on his face before he dropped into a stark mask of indifference. Shaking his head, he straightened and addressed us.

"The Galla Guards have escaped. It's not safe for Ash to stay here alone," he said in an urgent tone. I quickly shuffled out of bed and grabbed my boots. After slipping them on, I threw a grey knit sweater over my thin, white nightgown.

Patrick was much slower to get out of bed but still moved with equal shock. I averted my eyes from his half-dressed frame and flexed muscles. I felt too much shame to eye the proof of what we were doing just moments before. With Maverick's wince still fresh in my mind, I couldn't help but feel like Patrick was wrong; I couldn't have freedom in *all* things. My actions and impulses had consequences.

We loaded onto the community transport and rushed to the warehouse. Cyler ordered me to remain close to Jacob about ten times during the trip. His overprotectiveness was in overdrive, and his eyes swept out the window, as if prepared for a surprise attack at any moment.

As we pulled up, Huxley got out first and sprinted to the warehouse entrance where there was a slumped over figure on the dirt ground outside. Huxley halted and bent over to inspect it. Everyone except Jacob began slowly exiting the transport after him, each producing various sized knives. Maverick moved with speed and purpose towards whatever caused Huxley to pause .

"Stay in the transport, Ashleigh," Cyler ordered while clicking the lock. His lips were fixed firmly in a bleak line as he slid the door shut and made his way towards the others. His tense movements and shifting eyes made the shadows seem threatening.

Jacob grabbed my hand and squeezed. "Don't look, Ash," he whispered, but my eyes remained against the glass pane of the window, with my nose stubbornly pushed against it.

Patrick illuminated the dark exterior of the warehouse with a flick of a switch, and I went rigid with fear. The slumped object in the shadows was a too-still body cloaked with blood. It was contorted in an awkward shape, arms and legs bent in unnatural positions. I sucked in a shrill scream and bit the inside of my cheek to stop the fear from creeping out of my clenched mouth. My free fingers pinched my thigh. I wanted to be strong, but the sight was traumatizing.

Maverick bent over to inspect the body and shook his head. The grave movement confirmation to what I already knew— whoever it was, was dead.

"It's Kindle," Jacob said, reminding me that he

was with me in the transport and that I wasn't agonizing alone. "Fuck, I should have been here."

I briefly remembered running into Kindle the night of the Summer Solstice, mentally assigning a face to the brutal death before us.

"Was anyone else guarding the warehouse?" I asked, worried that there would be other casualties. I itched to ignore Cyler's command and go to them.

"No, we didn't have more to spare," Jacob replied honestly. "Between guarding the mines and the train station, we don't have enough people to cover everything, and Cyler refuses to allow women to take up any shifts."

Guilt gathered in the pit of my stomach. While I was off enjoying the best birthday of my life, the Dormas leadership council was preoccupied, leaving Dormas vulnerable. I let silent tears fall from my eyes. I didn't want to make this about me, but couldn't help but feel cursed.

Jacob grabbed my hand and squeezed. With great effort, I pulled my eyes away from the window and Kindle's lifeless form. When our eyes connected, I saw that Jacob, too, had unshed tears in his eyes and a shadowy expression on his handsome face.

"I was supposed to be on guard tonight," he quivered with a shaky voice while throwing a somber gaze back towards the body. I wrapped my arms around him and held him while he shook. He fell apart in my arms, and I felt his pounding intensity against my skin.

"It's not your fault," I murmured over and over into his slumped over and defeated form. "Jacob, it's not your fault."

Jacob wore guilt like a glove. He absorbed fault whenever possible, and I worried what the ramifications of Kindle's death would have on him long-term.

Kindle's death had a sobering effect on me—on all of us. A puncturing depression devoured me, and guilt like a vice gripped my heart. I was reminded that trivial things like birthdays or midnight almost-kisses are nothing when you're fighting for your life.

CHAPTER EIGHT

Maverick was meticulous in combing the warehouse for clues left behind by the escaped Galla guards. Ultimately, they left virtually nothing behind to show how they escaped. However, Maverick was able to piece together that they learned the limitations of their disease, and how to calm down enough to get away without sleeping. Once they saw a change in the routine, they made their escape by stealing Kindle's key card and killing him.

Huxley sent word to Mia to keep an eye out for the escaped guards, but most likely, they *calmly* fled to Galla with the hopes that they would find someone that could cure Maverick's manufactured illness.

To be safe, Cyler demanded that I spend the next few days at the Black Manor. Maverick kindly delivered my baked goods to Lois and Mark at the General Store, and they sent back more toys for me to paint during my involuntary time at the manor.

Since Jules moved out, the house was peaceful, but there was an edge about everyone that made tensions high. The guys mourned the loss of one of their citizens, and they approached work with a revitalized energy. They took on additional projects and rarely slept .

Kindle's funeral was a moderate affair, and only a handful of people showed up. It seemed that the town was too used to loss, and there wasn't any time to pause and mourn one of their own. Those that *did* attend merely nodded their head and said, "How unfortunate," before going back to work.

I was frozen by how desensitized Dormas was to death. How much loss had they endured to have such a diluted reaction to it?

Low-grade grief mellowed everyone out. Jacob tangled the grief and guilt harder than most. He mostly walked around with a half-smile that was heavy with the pain we all felt. It dissolved the playfulness in his eyes and hid away his flirty nature. Maverick completely avoided the house and was spending late nights at the Clinic. I didn't know how close they were to Kindle, but I did know that we all felt somewhat responsible for his passing.

What if we hadn't celebrated my birthday?

What if Jacob didn't trade his shift?

These lingering thoughts consistently ran on loop through my mind, attacking me in the vulnerable moments I sought happiness. And if I wasn't thinking about Kindle's dead body, I was obsessing over my almost-kiss with Patrick. The ricochet of emotions had me feeling sad, guilty, happy, and confused. Patrick and I hadn't had a moment to discuss what happened, so I felt unsure about where we stood. I purposely sought out his gaze in the rare moments we saw one another, but he avoided me. Was he second guessing everything?

By the fourth day of keeping locked up in the Black Manor, I was filled with anxiousness and demanded that Cyler lift his rules about me leaving the house. I knew that he was merely cautious, but I couldn't help but feel suffocated in the vast, empty home while the guys worked night and day.

"Fine!" Cyler huffed while carelessly spinning a knife on the kitchen island. "I still think we should wait till we are absolutely sure Lackley and Josiah aren't planning anything, but Lois has been up my ass asking about you. That is one damn persistent woman." He chuckled after discarding the knife and flipping through the morning news on his tablet and sipping his pitch black coffee.

I beamed when I learned that I would be allowed to return to my usual duties. In fact, I was so excited, that I kissed Cyler on the cheek before skipping out of the room and catching Patrick's forced smile. It was the first burst of happiness I'd felt since Kindle's passing, and I allowed it to flow throughout me.

I dressed in what had become my usual attire since moving to Dormas. Despite my modest habitual preferences, I liked the bright colors and slightly revealing nature of the dresses fashionable here. In Galla, my clothes reflected how repressed I felt; here, my style reflected freedom. I wore a teal form-fitting skirt that went all the way down to my ankles and paired it with a white shirt that hung off my shoulder and flowed freely around my torso.

During my walk to the general store, I spotted a familiar white head of hair and matching black attire —Mia. A small gaggle of women surrounded her. Upon further inspection, I saw a malevolent Jules standing apart from the group with Becca. They looked like they were headed out to the gardens to work and were both wearing uncaring expressions.

Jules' snarl was so thick that I imagined foam forming at the corner of her lips.

"I don't see how they could let a scavenger within the Dormas borders. They're all a bunch of ruthless murderers," Jules sneered while crossing her thin arms. She was wearing a long, forest-green dress and was dripping with fine jewelry. The look felt jarring in comparison to the other Walker women standing around her. Did she wear that to work in the gardens?

"I heard a rumor that they drink the blood of their dead," Becca added in a less severe tone. Becca appeared to be latched to Jules' side, and I mourned the brief camaraderie we shared. It was evident that she was now one of Jules' flunkies .

"Wanna find out if it's true?" Mia asked with a hard frown causing Becca's eyes to widen. Mia stood proudly against them, and I noticed her fingers twitching. The slight fidgeting of her hand reminded me of her knife throwing aptitude, and I quickly stepped up to stop the confrontation from escalating.

"Good Morning, ladies. It's a beautiful day, isn't it?" I asked loudly while breathing in the fresh morning air, diverting their attention to me. Jules crossed her thin arms over her chest. I noticed that she was significantly sunburned from working in the gardens.

"Maybe for *you* . We have to prepare for harvest in this sticky heat," she complained while fanning herself.

"What an admirable job. You know, I heard that the harvest should be extra plentiful this year. Cyler mentioned we should have a Harvest festival. Maybe get the whole Providence to help then have a big celebration," I said excitedly with a large smile. I knew that Jules was mad about working in the gardens, but from what most of the other Walker women told me, it was a fairly fun job. They even took lunch breaks with the Miners, which had resulted in a lot of new relationships. "Kemper said that the apple orchard—" I started before Jules cut me off.

"Save it. We've got to go. I just wanted to make sure this Scavenger knew that she wasn't welcome here, despite what my ignorant brothers may say."

Her prejudice was frustrating. "Well, I guess you *are* the expert on not being welcome," I replied with a sarcastic shrug, causing everyone's mouths to gape open at me. Apparently, it was no secret how Jules stumbled upon harvest duty, but it wasn't necessarily something brought up in polite company. Word travels fast in a small Providence, and I'm sure everyone would soon be gossiping about how Jules Black was put in her place by a mere Walker.

Mia gave Jules a sinister smile, spurring the group to move along. I watched them walk away and again wondered when I became such an outspoken person. Once they were out of earshot, Mia whirled around and graced me with a beautiful, genuine smile .

"My little *Agrio* to the rescue!" Mia gushed while looping her arm around mine. I felt terrible that Jules and her mini gang were bullying her.

"Jules is a petulant bully. We're thankful to have your tribe join us in Dormas," I said before I could stop myself. When did I start using "we" and "us" to describe the Dormas Leadership Council? I shook away the questions and conflict that plagued me.

"What brings you here?" I asked.

"We had three more infected Walkers drift about six miles outside of our tribal center. We decided to move up our migration plans. I came with the first half of the group; the second half will join us in two suns. Tallis doesn't fully trust the vaccination. If we're honest, he doesn't trust much of anything emperorLackley has touched." I couldn't help but agree with Tallis' distrust of the Empire. "Besides,"

Mia continued, "when word got to us that the Galla Guards escaped, Tallis felt that we needed to honor our end of the deal and provide some assistance."

"He seems like a good leader," I said, not willing to discuss Kindle's death and the Galla Guard's escape much further. Those lingering thoughts still preyed on me.

"He gets his best ideas from me." She wiggled her white eyebrows. "Besides, I'm happy to spend some time with my little *Agrio!* " She squealed in a high-pitched voice that seemed foreign coming out of her warrior-like body. "I've missed you. I feel like we're kindred souls out here in the outer rim of the empire. Plus, I wanted to hear if Huxley manned up and kissed you yet." She winked at me.

Her statement caused me to trip over myself and fall flat on my face. Literally. I kissed the dirt floor of the city walk until Mia manhandled me back up to a standing position with her bright but wicked smile.

Her question brought on a slew of memories I wasn't willing to analyze yet. I couldn't help but remember the ghost of a kiss Patrick whispered over my lips. I wondered if Huxley would be gentle, or if he would kiss me the same way he spoke to me. Harsh. Passionate. Intentional. I blushed which caused Mia to appraise me with an amused grin.

"I know that look," she said with a wink. "Hell, I *invented* that look." Mia clicked her tongue three times while her eyes stabbed every inch of my insecurities. I felt my cheeks grow hot with embarrassment. It was still weird to think about her and Huxley together.

After squirming under her observation, Mia squealed. "So you *do* like Huxley!"

"Don't say that out loud!" I whisper-shouted at her while glancing around to make sure no one overheard us. I nervously wiped sweat from my brow.

"Why not?" she replied in yet another loud voice while skipping back down the street. Her white hair bounced with each step.

I was about to explain that Huxley couldn't know what was happening, but then quickly shut my mouth. Why couldn't I talk about it? With Josiah, I had to repress all my desires, but here, nothing was holding me back. I was allowed to like someone or even feel attraction. Here, I wasn't unworthy of anyone.

"Okay, fine. Yes. I think Huxley is ridiculously handsome when he broods. When I'm not thinking about his frowning lips, I'm thinking about the way Cyler hugs me, or how Jacob holds my hands. How Patrick says my name, or how Kemper is perfect at everything, and how I want to soothe all that tortures Maverick. I think about all of them, Mia. More than I should." Mia stopped backward-skipping to gape at me. We silently stood in the street until she broke out in uncontrollable laughter.

"You're a true Dormas woman now!" she bellowed, causing me to cringe. "When I named you *Agrio* I had no idea just how *wild* you were! Get it, girl!!" She held up her hand for a high five but slowly lowered it when I merely stared at her in confusion.

"Come on, aren't you just a little excited? You've got, hold up, I need to count." She started ticking off names on her fingers, "...four, five, SIX men! That's gotta be a record somewhere!"

Mia's flippant attitude made me smile, and she rewarded me with a slap on the shoulder. Her tiny frame concealed her strength well and, once again, I stumbled, almost falling until she caught me and firmly righted my frame.

"Yes, yes, well this is all very exciting, but you forget," I said while rubbing my shoulder and neck. "I might be attracted to them, but there's no guarantee that one of them, let alone all of them, return those feelings. They're firm in their resolve to treat me like a sister." Well, maybe not Patrick—there was definitely nothing sisterly about what happened between us. "Not to mention, we're on the brink of war, and I'm still finding my way out of Josiah's shadow." Saying what truly bothered me caused a fierce melancholy to dig its tendrils down deep into my chest.

Mia slowed her pace, and her mocking expression morphed into something that resembled understanding. Her pale arm snaked around mine. Her fingers lightly dug into my skin, causing me to stop and stare at her.

"Huxley told me about Josiah," Mia said with sad eyes. I opened my mouth to ask her when, how, and why but she held up a hand to cut me off. "Huxley's my best friend; we tell each other *everything* —get used to it. I know that you definitely shouldn't worry about any of them liking you, hell, those boys are half way to being in *love* with you. As for the war, now is the perfect time to act on whatever feelings you have, because tomorrow isn't guaranteed."

She squeezed my arm harder and peered at me with sad, yet stoic eyes. "And Josiah? You should probably figure that out, and soon, because it's no longer just *your* heart on the line."

I remained quiet and let each revelation wash over my consciousness. Some part of me knew that, no matter what, this limbo would crash and burn.

We couldn't continue to tiptoe over the line. The small touches, the hugs, the cuddling... it would all eventually lead to something more. I just needed to learn how to navigate this with care. Mia was right; there was a lot at stake. Not only was my heart on the line, but their cohesiveness as a group was, too.

Mia and I ended up spending the day at the General store, where after some curious stares and questions, Lois welcomed her with open arms and a ton of work. We both spent hours giggling over the guys while painting toys for the Walker children.

CHAPTER NINE

The next day, I woke with a renewed spirit. Kindle's death and my guilt still lingered, but I felt a new purpose about everything. I decided that my first step in reasserting myself meant that I needed to overcome my reservations about the clinic and visit Maverick.

Like the others, Maverick had been distant since the Guard's escape and Kindle's death. I felt his patient, martyred coldness deeper than the others, even more so than Jacob, and I was determined to find out why.

So much had changed since Maverick and I guided that Walker woman to her death, and I still felt the pull of grief and sadness whenever I got near the cumbersome clinic. Maverick and I bonded deeply the last time I ventured here. I learned of his selfless heart, and I watched his sobering disenchanted views about death. He approached her passing like a frequent spectator of grief.

Once inside the Clinic, I shouted for Maverick but heard no response. After swallowing a few gulps of courage, I began making my way towards the back room where it all began. Where it all ended .

I passed the room where the Walker woman took her last breath, and I shuddered. The room was vacant and silent, but still felt filled to the brim with the presence of her.

Once I made my way further down the hallway, I noticed a cracked door and a bright, manufactured blue light seeping and splintering through the edges. I made my way there and opened the door. Inside, Maverick was sitting in an overstuffed office chair in front of six large screens, each projecting different codes and models of what appeared to be twisting ladders. He had headphones over his ears. I carefully took a broad path, so as not to startle him.

Once he saw me, he ripped off the headphones and appraised me with wide, frantic eyes. "Ash! What's wrong, what's going on? Are you hurt?" He got up and grabbed my shoulders and made quick work of inspecting every square inch of me. His broad palms ran down my arms and over my hips in a rushed examination. I briefly reveled in his close contact before distancing myself.

"What are you talking about? I'm fine. I just came to visit you," I explained with a half-smile. I realized the awkwardness of showing up unannounced and regretted bombarding him. Maverick exhaled in brief relief before scrutinizing me again. His brow sunk, and his dark eyes appraised me in concern.

"You never come to the Clinic, not since, well—not since the Walker woman died." Maverick looked down at his feet, as though contemplating telling me something. His kind eyes rose to meet mine, and I saw a sad resolve within his gaze that made my breath stall. "I meant to tell you; I finally was able to pull her file from Galla and learn her name—Rose. Her name was Rose Jamison," he said solemnly. I admired Maverick at that moment. Despite everything going on, he went through the trouble of finding a name for the nameless.

"That's a beautiful name," I whispered. Maverick nodded his head in response and looked at the floor.

"What brings you here, Ash?" He motioned for me to sit in his office chair. I plopped down, and he leaned against his desk next to me. He wore a deep maroon shirt tucked into tan pants that clung tightly to his frame.

"You've been detached lately. I've wanted to talk to you since the night Kindle died. But I haven't seen you," I explained. Maverick plucked a brightly colored rubber band that sat on his wrist. It snapped loudly against his skin, and I ached to rub away the sting of it.

"I don't mean to be distant, Ash. I've just got a lot on my mind. I'm sorry you felt like you had to come here to get my attention."

"That's not why I came here, Maverick," I tried to explain. "I'm here because I—I miss you." Maverick's eyes lingered on the far wall. I ached to see his wistful eyes, but instead was swarmed with his sullen speculation.

Once again, Maverick slapped the rubber band against his wrist, and I immediately clawed my way out of the chair and grabbed it from him, causing it to ping against my own fingers.

After a long, uncomfortable silence, Maverick spoke. "Dad was convinced he wouldn't catch influenza X. We took all the necessary precautions. Moving the town away from the infected. Burning the deceased. He researched every aspect of X in every controlled environment imaginable. And yet, without reason, he started to develop the white-hot blisters on his body," Maverick's large hand grasped his chest. It seemed his words were causing him physical pain.

"He locked himself in the Clinic, and I knew. I—I knew what it was but didn't say anything to anyone. I guess I was still too shocked to accept the truth." Maverick's voice stumbled over his words, and he started to speak at a faster rate, as though he was desperate to toss out the heartbreak and emotions that consumed him.

"Then, he succumbed to the last phase of the illness; he truly became a Walker. We have an alarm for when an infected Walker is spotted in the Providence. It lets everyone know to go inside until the threat had passed. It's an effective system, intended to diminish the spread of the disease," he said in a methodical manner, and I clung to every syllable Maverick said .

"The next morning when the bell rang throughout the town center, I knew it was him wandering the streets. My mother was beside herself. Before any of us could stop her, she ran to him and embraced him with a hug and kiss. I—I don't think I'll ever get the image of her frail arms wrapped around his bloody body out of my mind," Maverick said. His words shook, and he pinched his arm as he spoke.

"She ended his life by stabbing him in the gut with my uncle's blade, to end his suffering; it was a truly selfless act. Within three days, the first sores began to develop on her own skin, and she ended her life." Maverick peered down at his shoes, but his gaze was elsewhere.

"I never told Cyler or Jules that I knew—that I could have stopped Mom from going to him. That I could have been the one to ease his suffering. I was too ashamed. Our Mother did what I couldn't. She accepted his fate and ran out to join him in death."

Tears began to fall down my cheeks as I absorbed Maverick's story. "I'm so sorry, Maveric," I said, sobbing while wondering how deep his mother's love was for his father. Would I have had the courage to end someone's life?

"I'm far too familiar with death, Ash," Maverick whispered.

I approached him like one would a wild animal—with caution and respect. After maneuvering myself between his opened, outstretched legs, I rested my head against his thudding heart. My arms instinctively wrapped around him, and after a moment's pause, he returned my hug with care.

"I'm determined to finish my father's work. To replicate the cure and free our Providence from the Empire's clutches. I want to mass produce the cure, I want to completely eradicate X," he growled with a resolve that I felt in my bones. "When Kindle was murdered, it reminded me that there is no time for distractions, there's too much at stake." His words sank through me like lead, and I immediately distanced myself.

I was the distraction he spoke of. It was *my* birthday he was attending when Kindle was murdered and the Galla Guards escaped. I took two giant steps backward to distance myself from the blow of his words. My mind collapsed into an agonized womb of consciousness. I understood Maverick's feelings and wholeheartedly agreed that he should focus on finding the cure, but I still felt sad. It didn't mean that I couldn't feel sorrow or even longing. It just meant that now was not the time to act upon it.

"What's going on in that beautiful mind of yours?" He stretched out his arm to touch the side of my face, but I distanced myself more, avoiding his touch.

"I care for you, Maverick. For all of you. And I'm no stranger to patience. I understand what you need to do; I respect what you need to do. But I don't have to like it. I don't have to sit here and pretend that I'm okay with you distancing yourself from me," I said while wrapping my arms around my midsection as if to hold the emotions I felt at bay. "I'm not asking for your undivided attention. I'm just asking for a sliver of it. Don't push me away. Let me help you." I felt the pangs of rejection attach themselves into my confidence.

"You're not the distraction I spoke of, Ash. At least, not in the way you're thinking," Maverick bit out with worried eyes. Once again, he reached for me, but this time I allowed his fingers to grab onto my arms.

"Jealousy is a distraction. Repressing my feelings for you, is a distraction." His words washed over me, and I scooted closer. "I care for you, Ashleigh, probably more than I should. I just need to work on it all. It feels like there's never enough time." Maverick's intensity consumed me, and I yearned to explore the possibilities of his intentions with me.

This subtle switch in the dynamic between us was still very new, and I was more than willing to wait it out and let it evolve on its own terms. I was just happy to know that I wasn't the only one feeling this anticipation, this craving.

"As far as helping me," he said, "I'm glad you offered. I was hoping to use a sample of your blood. Since you have natural immunity, we might be able to use it to figure out the last element to the vaccine." The sudden shift in topics gave me whiplash, and I shook my head to rid myself of the dazed possibilities in his previous words.

He gently grabbed my shoulders and directed me to face the computer monitors. Models of different objects and gene sequences scrolled vertically on the screen, and occasionally an alert would pop up, indicating that something of importance was discovered.

"I'm so close, Ash," he murmured while watching the various codes roll around like digital waves on his screen. His eyes scanned the confusing figures, seeking out the answers to this terrible disease.

"I'll help. I'll do whatever you need," I replied honestly and with more force than necessary. I rolled up my sleeve and held out my thin arm to Maverick which made him chuckle.

"Well, alright then. I don't usually keep blood draw kits in my pocket, so you'll have to wait a minute. I would do this in the main room, but, uh— "

I cut him off. "I'm fine wherever, Maverick. This Clinic is a part of you. I . . . I want to be a part of that. Of you."

Maverick looked at me with such awe and respect that my eyes watered. He lifted his hand and scratched his head, causing his red-brown hair to ruffle. "Well, okay then, lets uh—let's go," he choked out.

After Maverick drew my blood, he spent more time half-heartedly explaining to me his research while he held my hand. When he spoke, his eyes lit up with such hope that I, too, saw a future where the X vaccine was accessible and Walkers didn't exist. A future where the world wasn't upon his shoulders. A future where we could maybe be *more* .

CHAPTER TEN

Josiah 16 Years Ago

Father dragged me to the Walker auctions at the first hint of morning light. My mother refused to attend. She usually had a headache until mid-afternoon on the nights Father hosted dinner parties, and last night emperorLackley visited, so it would be at least a week before she recovered. Father was particularly eager to attend this Walker auction, I noticed. He happily munched on his breakfast while describing to me the perks of owning a Walker.

"All respectable families own Walkers these days, it's simply a *necessity* ," he said while crumbs of bagel tumbled out of his puffy cheeks and onto the floor of the transport. Father was always messy, and Mother was always scolding him for it.

"I thought we had to stay away from the Walkers, Father?" I questioned while watching him lick cream cheese from the tips of his pudgy fingers. He scooted backward in his leather seat and pulled on the tight seat buckles that contained his thick frame.

"Yes, well, these Walkers either have immunity or are willing to trade themselves in exchange for the vaccine. But they're still trash; unworthy of the space they take up. Understand that, boy?"

I nodded in understanding. My eight-year-old mind soaking up every bit of wisdom my father shared.

Father's tablet rang. He answered it and began arguing with whoever was on the other side of the call. He was always arguing with someone. Especially Mother. One might even say that it's his favorite pastime. I noticed that he got a certain gleam in his eyes whenever she cowered from him.

We continued to travel towards the auction, and I pressed my nose against the cold transport window to see my surroundings better. I found the Walker Zones had just enough mystery and horror to keep my imaginative mind occupied until the transport parked itself and the doors slid open.

The building where the Walker Auction was, stood out like a beacon of newness in the rundown Zone. It was ten stories tall and covered in screens that flashed different faces of Walkers hoping to be purchased. The lawn was manicured and the windows shiny but surrounded by run-down shacks with barefoot children running along the road.

Despite being vaccinated, attendants handed us mouth coverings that slipped over our ears and plastic gloves intended for our hands. Mother always said that you could never be too careful when it came to Influenza X and the nasty Walkers, so I readily accepted them.

I sat quietly by my father and watched a dozen Walkers stroll onto the metal stage. Their specifications were listed methodically, and one by one, each Walker was auctioned off to the highest bidder. They each wore resigned but hopeful expressions. I tried to focus during the entire ordeal, but still found the auction to be incredibly boring. Father was always chastising my inability to sit still.

Most of the Walkers were bought, but a few still left the stage in defeat. No one wanted them as servants, which meant they would have to continue on without the vaccine.

After the stage cleared, I wondered why Father

didn't bid on any of the available Walkers. Plenty of them seemed fine enough, but he remained quiet. Some of the crowd cleared but a few remained. I fidgeted with my coat sleeve and father pinched my arms to keep me still. "Stop fidgeting," he whispered while grabbing me harder.

A tall and slender woman with red hair strolled towards the middle of the stage. The woman smiled at everyone still in the auditorium and even winked at a few. She wore an emerald gown that dragged upon the floor as she walked.

"Masters and Mistresses, we have an extraordinary treat for you all today." She gestured towards the side of the stage where a girl that looked to be about half of my very experienced eight years, was being guided into the bright spotlight next to the fiery-haired woman. The young girl had fuzzy hair and a baggy dress that barely hid how skinny she was.

I noticed Father perk up, and I, too, watched with interest. There was something special about this girl, something that caught Father's attention, as well as the focus of the rest of the room, and I wanted to know what.

"There is more than meets the eye to this little Walker Girl. She's immune to X." Several gasps could be heard around the room. Even I knew that Immunity to X was rare, she wouldn't require a vaccine. "She was found clinging to her dead mother and father two days ago in the Walker Zones. It was a very tragic discovery, as you can well imagine." The woman smiled as she patted the little girl's head, and I wondered what made her so happy. I looked around and saw that, like my father, everyone seemed to hold their breath at what the woman had to say next.

"Immunity in a Walker is rare, as I'm sure you all know. It shows that she has good breeding. She also will not be needing the vaccine. Because of that, we will start the bidding at five thousand Drachmas."

Whispers and murmurs erupted, and I once again looked around the room to see everyone's reaction when a thick, meaty hand slapped down on my knee. "Pay attention," my father hissed. I ached to rub the sting away but didn't want to anger him further—Father's anger wasn't to something I wanted to test. So instead, I peered at the sad-looking Walker on the stage .

The announcer clicked her tongue and stared out into the crowd until everyone went silent again. "Let the bidding begin," she said in a sing-song voice.

The woman slowly maneuvered the various

amounts of money thrown her way, and as the number rose, I fought the urge to snap my head around to see who was offering each amount.

7,000

10,000

12,000

"Fifteen thousand Drachmas!" my father's voice bellowed across the room, causing shocked silence to inflate around us. An attendant walked towards him, carrying a metal case, and my father placed the tip of his greasy thumb upon the scanner to unlock it. The box was then opened, revealing stacks of gold sheets. Father waved his arms, presenting the ridiculously large sum of money towards the crowd.

"SOLD!" the woman replied with a clap and a broad grin. The young girl flinched, and I laughed at her skittishness. Girls were so weak.

We traveled to a back room behind the stage. My father was directed to sign a thick stack of papers as he spoke to the woman. "An immune Walker is rare. My colleagues will be jealous," Father said gleefully.

"Oh yes, you definitely will be the talk of the Providence. emperorLackley himself is the only other man within two hundred miles to own an immune Walker." The woman gave us a broad grin, and I noticed her red lipstick stuck to her pearly-white teeth.

"While you read through the last of the papers, I'll attach your tag. It's microchipped, so you'll know where she is at all time. Some people shave the sides of their Walker's head so it's fully visible, but it's a personal preference, of course," the woman said while producing a white handheld machine. She walked over to the Walker and forced her to lay down on an end table.

"This will only hurt a bit dearie." Her voice was overly chipper while she slipped the Walker's ear through two of its prongs. " Prepare yourselves, sirs, they tend to scream a lot," she whispered to Father and I. He rolled his eyes, but I clamped down hard to prevent any screams from creeping through.

"One, two, and...," the woman said before a hissing noise with a loud clip erupted through the room. The little girl started whimpering and released a gasp. She didn't scream, but I noticed how her face slipped into a look of agony.

The woman wiped a few drops of blood from the Walker's cheek, then scanned the bronze tag cuffed to the outer ridge of her ear. "You're strong," the woman noted. "Good, you'll need it," I heard her whisper while peering up at Father.

"Yes, well, there we have it. I've sent her digital signal to you. She's all yours," the woman said at a normal volume with a smile. Father continued to read over the paperwork and his legal obligations.

I took advantage of his distraction and went over to the Walker, who seemed frozen. She briefly touched the brass clip permanently attached to her ear and scrunched her eyes closed in sadness.

"Uh—Hi, I'm Josiah," I said in a low voice. Although Father's earlier words about Walker's unworthiness were still fresh in my mind, the curiousness of the little girl didn't escape me. Mother always says I must introduce myself to everyone. "What's your name?"

"Ashleigh." Her voice was small, timid. Her eyes, red from days of crying. I remembered that her mother and father died. "Wh-why was everyone f-fighting over me?" she asked with a squeak. I glanced back at my father then stepped closer to her. She seemed sad and broken and for some reason, I wanted to fix it.

"Because you look like a princess," I answered in a hushed tone. Her smile made Father's open-palmed slap across my pale cheek almost worth it.

CHAPTER ELEVEN

Ashleigh - Present Day

Maverick and I developed a routine of walking to the Clinic together and sharing breakfast as the sun rose, while he observed his overnight analytics. Knowing that Maverick would crawl into his office and work himself to death gave me the resolve to keep him company despite my heavy eyelids.

I didn't stay long this morning. The bakery was closed in observance of Pioneer day, and I wanted to walk around town. Besides, Maverick caught a lead on a particularly tricky gene and was so submersed in studying it that even my breathing was too loud for him. I saw his need to be alone and readily gave it to him.

Pioneer day was a holiday that recognized Cyler, Maverick, and Jules' parents for their contributions to the Providence. I think the festive holiday was partly to blame for Maverick's intensity. Although I wished I could comfort him, I knew his coping mechanism, although not necessarily healthy, was work.

As I walked around the square, I saw men joyfully chatting amongst one another. The mine and gardens were closed, so everyone took advantage of the freedom and beautiful weather. I recognized some of the Walker women that regularly frequented my Bakery. They happily spoke to one another and once again I wished I could form a deeper bond with them. I was thankful to be in the Black Manor, but I wish I could get to know and connect with some of my fellow Walkers.

I spotted Cyler and Jules at the end of the road and walked towards them. Mark Caverly, the General Store owner, was talking their ears off. I saw a proud smile on Jules' face, but Cyler seemed to slump under the attention. As I got closer, I heard bits of their conversation.

"I met your father when he was just a wee boy!" Mark exclaimed with a chuckle. "He was always giving your grandmother a run for her money. He used to strip down naked in the square and piss on the sidewalk. Of course that was in the old town, before we had to relocate," Mark said pensively while Jules let out a single hollow, laugh.

"Ah and your mother was a beautiful woman. She had many suitors but only your father caught her eye—that was before relationships *diversified,* of course," he said with a wink. "She had a big heart. There was never a stray in Dormas, and everyone always had a home at the Black Manor. They both would be so proud."

I noticed unshed tears in Jules' eyes. She looked vulnerable and young in that moment. I often forgot that she, too, had lost loved ones. Once she saw me standing near, all tenderness fled her expression and disgust took its place.

"Hello, Happy Pioneer Day," I greeted. Cyler turned to look at me, and I saw the sadness behind his polite smile. Today was difficult.

"Thanks, babe," Cyler whispered. I noticed Mark grin and whisper to the man next to him at Cyler's sweet nickname for me. Jules huffed and turned to walk away without sparing me even a glance, but in her brash brush-off, she ran smack dab into a shirtless Tallis. She gasped.

"Well hello there, Jules," Tallis said with a grin. "You've got to stop bumping into me, some will start to think you're doing it on purpose."

Jules laughed nervously while peering around at us. Mark Caverly looked stunned to see the Scavenger chief, and the entire Providence went quiet with curiosity. Jules emitted a nervous laugh. "I have no idea what you're talking about. Move out of my way," she ordered.

Tallis looked at Jules like she was a challenge he just accepted. His bright, wild eyes glistened with promise. He took a crooked finger and traced Jules' elbow before bending over and whispering loud enough for me to hear. "You first."

Jules scoffed at him, hiked up her dress, and then maneuvered herself around him after spitting in the dirt at his bare feet and cursing.

"Well that was interesting," I murmured. Cyler closed the distance between us, ignoring his baby sister's tantrum.

Tallis nodded in greeting towards us before making his way over to a group of chatting miners and Scavengers. The integration had a few prejudice bumps in the road, but it had mostly been smooth. Tallis moved with confidence, and his exotic features made the chatting Walker womens' eyes grow wide with curiosity.

"You'll have to excuse me, Mr. Caverly. It seems the person I was looking for found me." Cyler hooked my arm through his and began walking down the street, diverting my attention from Tallis. People seemed to want to stop and chat with Cyler, probably providing commentary on his parents, but each time they got close, he leaned in to me and acted as though we were having a serious conversation.

"I'm sorry, babe. I'll let you go once we get out of here," he murmured as another man tried to approach us. We made our way towards the manor, but instead of going inside, Cyler directed me around the left side of the house towards a section of thick trees.

Once under the shady protection of the forest, Cyler released my hand and rested his forehead against one of the trunks. "Maverick gets to hide in his Clinic. Jules simply basks in the glow of the attention. Where does that leave me?" he asked while twisting his body and sliding down the trunk until he was sitting at the base. Cyler's lips were pressed together, his dark eyes narrowed in frustration .

"Do you want to talk about it?" I asked. Cyler

always seemed in control of his emotions. I could easily gauge what the others needed, but with him I felt unsure.

"One day, I want to tell you all about them. Mom would have loved you. She'd probably be arranging a marriage between us by now." He chuckled. "I got my determined stubbornness from her. Dad would be running this Providence much better than I've done." Cyler lifted one shoulder in a tentative half-shrug. "But I want to hide away today. Can we do that? I need a distraction."

I wanted to argue with him. Cyler's entire life was one big distraction. He worked himself to the bone, constantly shifting from one problem to the next, struggling to continue his parents' legacy while avoiding grief. I wanted to urge him to confront his problems but had enough sense to recognize that now wasn't the time.

"I'll never get used to the trees here," I said in an obvious attempt at changing the subject. "I used to think Galla was beautiful with all the tall, uniform, buildings. But now that I've seen the wild of the trees, I don't think Galla can even compare." I looked up at the large shaded leaves above us. Bursts of sunlight peeked through the gaps of the branches, causing beams of light to sprinkle across us.

Cyler smiled broadly, and a mischievous look replaced his grim frown. "I want to show you something. Are you up for a little exploring?" Cyler asked while standing back up. He dusted off his pants, grabbed my hand, and started pulling me towards the manor.

"I'm up for an adventure," I replied with a smile.

We made our way towards the back of the manor where a bright-blue canvas tarp covered a large bundle. Cyler removed it and revealed an odd looking contraption. It had two circular, black inflated pieces of thick, ridged rubber connected by a seat and what appeared to be handlebars. It was all black and intriguing.

"It's a motorcycle," Cyler explained. "The old world used it as transportation. Tires haven't been used in ages, but they make for a fun bumpy ride." He slid what appeared to be a small, metal ridged rod in a miniature port hole while mounting the seat. He pressed a leg down forcefully on a lever at the bottom and the machine roared to life. It sounded like a guttural growl and was steadfast with such intensity that I couldn't help but smile.

Cyler waved to me to join him, and I raised my merlot skirt above my knees while throwing my left leg over the seat. My feet rested on two protruding pegs on either side of the machine. I pressed close to Cyler, and he grabbed my hands, wrapping them around his abs. I felt the ridge of his muscles beneath the thin material of his black shirt. The closeness made me want to take advantage of his nearness and run my fingers along the crevasses of his muscles.

"Hold on, babe," Cyler said, and then we took off.

It took a moment to get used to the strange sensation. Wind pressed against me, and I learned to move with Cyler as we took each turn. He increased his speed once we hit a long strip of open space, and I squealed in delight, causing Cyler to shake in laughter. It felt truly freeing to be with him in that moment. Nothing else mattered.

As we traveled, I noticed a city in the distance. Grass and shrubs were overgrown, and metal buildings were scattered between the trees and plants. I realized instantly that this must be the old Dormas, before X hit and they had to relocate. Cyler drove through it, and I peered at the dead city with sadness. Cyler's rigid frame hinted that he, too, felt the ominous feel of the old town.

As he continued to drive, each bump in the road made me feel like I was going to fly off the contraption. Soon, we arrived at a large abandoned house that looked nearly identical to the Black Manor. He parked the motorcycle and we dismounted. My legs wobbled from the intense vibrations and the adrenaline. Cyler wordlessly led the way around the house and towards the back, while I followed and avoided the large shrubs that tickled my ankles.

Finally, we arrived at a large tree. A strip of wood that looked like a ladder was bolted to the tree's trunk.

"Time to climb, babe," Cyler instructed while stepping on the bottom ledge and ascending the incredibly large tree. I followed suit, despite the pounding fear within me. It wasn't the height that made me nervous. It was the sight of Cyler's flexing muscles as he gripped each ledge and how utterly alone we were.

I followed him, and by the time we reached the top, I was out of breath. Cyler pulled me through an open hatch, and I found myself standing on an enclosed platform. It was a small room within the canopy of the tree. Abandoned toys that were faded or rusted littered the floor, and I noticed a sign on one wall that said "No Girls Allowed" which made me grin in amusement.

I pointed to it. "Should I leave?" Cyler saw what was making me laugh and immediately chuckled.

"You're no girl, Ash. You're *all* woman," he said in a smoky tone that made me flush and the temperature increase by at least ten degrees. "My father and Kemper's grandfather built this for us. We had a lot of adventures here." Cyler chuckled while looking around. He had to crouch low, as the ceiling was about six feet tall. "Jules was always thinking of ways to sneak in."

I made my way over to a window and gasped. From here, I could see the tops of the trees. Sunlight danced along the leaves, and birds flew overhead. My sight stretched as far as the Deadlands, and I noticed a green haze in the air off in the distance.

"It's so beautiful, Cy," I whispered.

"I'm glad I could show you this." Cyler walked behind me and wrapped his arms around my stomach, pulling me close. This felt so *intimate,* almost like a date. Cyler and I were two magnets with an incredible pull.

"Thanks for coming here with me, Ash," Cyler said while trailing his fingers lower on my hips. He dug into my plush skin where my smoke-colored top had ridden up. I considered pushing my hips back in response to see if Cyler would push into me. If he would turn me around and kiss my aching lips.

"Cyler—I want . . .," I trailed off. Unsure of what

to say. I wanted him to kiss me. I wanted to feel him against my warm skin and trace his lips with my own. I desired it all.

I wasn't worried about the boundaries they'd drawn to protect their group. I wasn't thinking about the consequences, Josiah, or the fear and sadness. I didn't think about *anything*. My mind was a blank canvas, and I wanted Cyler to breathe color into my life.

Cyler sucked in a deep breath and gripped me tighter. I felt like molten lava, flowing with heat and destruction under his heavy, possessive hold. His lips kissed the spot under my ear, and I felt bumps of sensation trickle through every square inch of my body. His kisses traveled lower towards my collarbone.

"I know what you want, Ash," Cyler began between kisses. "And *fuck* I want to give it to you." One of his fingers dipped beneath the band of my skirt, and I gasped. It lingered dangerously close to the edge of all the things I wanted but couldn't have.

"I want to love every part of you. Kiss and lick your delicious skin until you're screaming my name." His words ignited a passion within me, and I squirmed under his hold. I tried to turn around and close the distance between us, but he held me steady, disallowing me to move. "I promise that I'll worship your body the way it deserves," he said while pulling me tighter against him. I felt his hardness against the curve of my butt, and heat pooled in my center. "But not until I speak with the others," he said with regret while pulling away from me.

The mention of the rest of the guys drenched my senses with shame. What was I doing? I slumped in embarrassment and put my hands over my face.

"Don't close off from me now, babe," Cyler begged. He grabbed my shoulders and turned me so that we were facing one another. "This," he said while pulling my hands from my face, "is just beginning. We *will* be together. Don't look ashamed or embarrassed, trust me."

"Okay, I trust you," I said, still feeling the effects of his stare.

"I just want to do this *right*. I want to go into this without any regrets. You don't deserve anything less."

We hurried out of the treehouse and rode back to Dormas. I felt confused but still exhilarated by my trip with Cyler. I was gifted with a glimpse into his life, and I clung to it. I just didn't know how to move forward, how to jump the line and free fall into my desires.

CHAPTER TWELVE

The General Store was rather busy this morning. The Walker women that worked in the gardens passed our shop daily, and all but Jules walked in to buy muffins or bread from me. If Jules wasn't pretending I didn't exist, she was gossiping to the other Walker women about me. Jules thrived on feeling important and belittling others. It made it challenging to build friendships outside of the guys.

Other than the occasional confrontation with Jules, my days slipped into a comfortable routine of spending spare minutes with Cyler, Jacob, Maverick, Patrick, Kemper, and sometimes, even Huxley—if he was in a good enough mood. When I wasn't at the Bakery, I was traveling between them, trying to assist where I could to ease some of their burdens. Cyler

refused to let me take a night watch shift at the ·
mines, but he couldn't stop me from bringing dinner
to the guys that *were* working.

I was constantly amazed by their tenacity. Cyler
acted as a diplomat, continually listening to the
problems of his citizens and finding compromises
between them. Jacob's work at the train station kept
the General Store well stocked, and he was always
scrounging the Empire for the best ingredients for
my creations at the Bakery. When Maverick wasn't
attempting to replicate the X vaccine, he ran a full-
fledged Clinic, where he saw at least two citizens a
day. Huxley and Patrick, although vastly different,
worked in the mines with seamless proficiency. Most
men in the Providence worked there, and they
found just the right line between being their superior and being their friend. Once a week, Huxley
ordered desserts from the Bakery to treat their
seventy-five workers. And Kemper? Kemper fixed
everything.

Today, Kemper set aside the entire day to fix the
Bakery's oven so that it was level, and that had me
bouncing with eager energy. I was so excited to
spend the whole day with him that I burned a whole
batch of chocolate chip muffins, as well as Lois'
patience. Like all of them, he was overworked. His

small team of builders were working overtime to get each Walker immigrant a cabin of their own.

When he wasn't building, he spent his evenings fixing things around the community. Last week, he built a ramp for one of the elderly community members that used a wheelchair. He coordinated so much but rarely took credit for it. Kemper simply saw a need and fulfilled it.

When he arrived, he looked tired but just as happy to see me as I was to see him. He wore tight denim that clung to his tall, slender, frame.

"Hey, Ashleigh," he said in a cheerful voice. He carried a forest-green toolbox that clanged with each step he took.

"Hey, Kemp, I've missed you." I walked into his open embrace. He nearly dropped his toolbox at the force of my hug.

"I should move my office closer to the town center, so I can see you more. These team builds and Providence repairs are brutal," he replied while letting me go and rubbing his forehead.

Brutal indeed. Aside from my mornings with Maverick, it felt nearly impossible to steal time away with any of them. If I wanted to see them, I had to roll up my sleeves and help.

"I cleared my day, though. I was hoping that

maybe after we get your oven situated, you could maybe teach me how to bake a cake? You know— since the one I made for your birthday was such a disaster." He gave me a deprecating grin that made me chuckle. "Of course, if you're busy or—or some- thing, I could, uh, leave."

"Spending the day with you sounds lovely, Kemp. And . . . it wasn't that bad. I'm just amazed that you managed to both undercook *and* overcook it. That takes true skill." Somehow Kemper had burned the exterior of the cake, but uncooked batter had still oozed from inside.

Kemper laughed, and we maintained a playful conversation between us while he worked on the oven. I watched him with giddy greedy eyes as he worked. He was methodical in the way he approached a problem. Examined it from every angle while biting his lip in concentration. His attentive- ness made me wonder if he approached *everything* with that much care.

Once he was done leveling the oven and cleaning it, he tinkered with a few other things that needed fixing in the Bakery; adjusting a sliding door, greasing a drawer. He inspected every inch of the Bakery until there was nothing left that needed improving.

"Are you done prolonging the inevitable?" I asked with a smile while pulling out the recipe for chocolate cake. Despite knowing it by heart, I wanted Kemper to reference it since it was his first time making it.

"I guess it's time to face my fears," he joked back.

I explained each step in painstaking detail and even told him why each of the various ingredients were important to the flavor of the dish, why following each step was vital to its success. Kemp studied me like I was a manual and even took notes while I spoke, never once asking me to hurry up or get on with it.

He mixed the batter with ease, and I watched the way his slender frame moved. His forearm flexed with each twist of his wrist and mix of the batter. I had to pry my eyes away from his graceful movements. Watching Kemper was addicting.

Once the cake was in the oven, we sat down and painted some of the toys left out by Lois. She was determined to get them completed this week, and once again, Kemper was eager to help.

"Are you regretting coming here on your day off?" I asked with a smirk while putting the finishing touches on a carved bear. "Don't let Lois know what all you fixed. She'll keep finding more work for you."

I chuckled. That woman was ruthless and loved having the Dormas Leadership Council around.

"It's worth it," he replied while painting a smile on a doll with such attentiveness that I wondered if he had any artistic abilities. It wouldn't surprise me; Kemper seemed to be able to do anything.

"Where did you learn how to build?" I asked

"My Grandfather taught me; he saw that I liked working with my hands, so when I was old enough to take direction, he gave me little projects that turned into bigger projects. Then I was building an entire town." Kemper set down the doll he was working on and peered at me with a sigh. "He died a year ago." Kemper's voice held such sadness and conviction that my heart ached. "He outlived his wife and my mom, survived X, survived the Eastern Scavenger attacks, all to just peacefully die in his sleep. He was a good man."

I reached out and grabbed his hand, then gave it a little squeeze, reminding him that I was here.

"Cyler and the others have always been my family. We're like brothers. But I still miss my Grandpa," he said in a choked voice.

"I'm sure he'd be proud of you," I replied, not knowing what to say.

Kemper coughed then grabbed another toy, his

gesture seemed to end the conversation, and we went back to painting in uncomfortable silence.

The beeping of the oven ended our torturous silence, and we both breathed a sigh of relief. He stood, walked over and opened the oven door slightly then said, "It needs a bit longer," before shutting it. He re-read over the recipe as I watched. Kemper was a perfectionist. Every action, every thought, every word was designed with such intention that I wondered if Kemper ever actually broke out of his carefully constructed comfort zone and walked on the careless side. I briefly remembered the others teasing him about streaking in the town center, but that was under the influence of alcohol.

"Kemp, do you ever let go?" I asked while standing and walking towards him.

"What do you mean?" He stopped looking at the cake and peered up at me in confusion. I knew what a lifetime of striving for perfection could do to a person. I knew how exhausting it could be.

"Do you ever . . . I don't know, act without think-ing?" I questioned, searching for the words.

"No, but lately it's all I can think about," he said quietly while biting his lip. "I want to forget the consequences, forget my responsibilities. Forget being perfect." He looked at me with such intensity I had to catch my breath.

Abandoning the cake in the oven, Kemper looked around the store, and after seeing no one, leaned close. He grabbed my hands and moved them around his waist before nuzzling my hair. "Like right now? I want to forget that we're in a public place," he said with an exhale. I felt his hands drift lower until they were wrapped around the back of my thighs. He lifted me up and placed me on the bakery counter. "I want to forget this beautiful dress you're wearing. I want to rip it to shreds," he said while tracing a finger down the buttons trailing the front of my dress. He froze at my chest. "I want to sink into the swells of your breasts. I want to drink you in. I want to burn a thousand cakes because we're too busy doing *other* things," he murmured.

The bell to the shop rang and he smiled while biting his lip. He drifted away from me then took the cake out of the oven with care. I watched his precise movements while I struggled to catch my breath. The corner of his lips lifted in amusement at my reaction to him.

He put a wooden toothpick in the batter and slid it out carefully to inspect if it was done, which it was, and he rewarded me with a tender smile. "I brought you something," he said. His large hands struggled to slip into the pockets of his too-tight jeans, causing me to chuckle and stare at his movements. I slid off the counter then coughed to expel the last bit of lust from my system.

"Ah, here it is!" He pulled out a singular blue-striped birthday candle. I grinned in response. He walked slowly towards me and grabbed my hand. "It bothered me that I ruined your birthday with my burnt-but-not-burnt cake," he admitted with a hard smile, then peered at me with unspoken sadness. We both knew his cake didn't ruin my day. Kindle's death and the guilt that followed is what made my birthday so grim. Nevertheless, I appreciated Kemper's attempt at a do-over. I sensed that he wanted to replace the bad memories with a new one.

"My grandfather taught me to have pride in everything I do. If he were alive, he would have told me to keep baking cakes until I got it right—especially if he knew it was for someone as beautiful and perfect as you."

Kemper continued while blushing, "So, Ash, wanna blow out the candle?" He puffed out a blast of air, and minty fresh breath wafted towards me, mixing in with the sweet chocolatey smell of the cake.

My chest rose and fell, and my breathing felt labored. I almost forgot that Kemp was waiting for me to answer.

"Yes, I'd love to," I replied while walking with him over to the counter. "And for the record . . ." I glanced at him from the corner of my eyes. "I liked your faulty cake. I prefer effort to results." It was important to me that he understood that I didn't expect perfection, especially after seeing his rebellious side just moments before. Now I found myself craving it.

Kemper smiled then, a genuine, heart-stopping smile. It brightened the entire room. While sliding the birthday candle into the spongy cake, he hummed then ignited the wick with a lighter he produced from his too-tight pockets.

"Happy Birthday, Ash," he whispered.

I blew out the candle and watched the smoke carry up my unspoken wish.

CHAPTER THIRTEEN

The Bakery was abnormally slow the next morning. Aside from the few stragglers and my breakfast regulars, there was an odd quiet about the General Store that had me on edge. Even Lois lacked her usual inquiring gaze.

I was wiping down the wooden countertop when a shrill siren erupted throughout the store and echoed on the streets. It sounded like a muffled, squealing pig and made me cover my ears.

"What is that?" I exclaimed to Lois who was practically running towards the windows to inspect what was happening. Three loud beeps sounded, and the sirens stopped.

"There's an infected Walker loose on the town," Lois said in an annoyingly giddy tone. She peered down her nose out the dusty window, and I followed suit. "When the alarm beeps three times, it means it's on the main strip. We might even see it!"

I was shocked by Lois' excitement over seeing a Walker, but she lived a relatively mundane life, so I assumed that any excitement was enjoyable to her, no matter how morbid.

"It's been a good eight months since we've had an infected Walker!" Mark exclaimed while scratching his stomach and adjusting his glasses so that he could have a better look, too.

I scanned as far as I could, and in the distance noticed a figure wobbling down the road, holding what appeared to be a bundle of blankets.

"What'll happen to the Walker?" I asked in a whisper, almost dreading the answer.

"Cyler or Huxley usually will shoot them with their bow. They're our most skilled marksmen, don't you know," Lois said with a grin.

"Right they are, dear. I'd almost say they're the best in the Empire, wouldn't you agree?" Mark candidly replied.

"Yes, yes. Most definitely." Lois nodded eagerly.

The Walker moved closer to us, and I noticed that it was a woman. Long, white, matted hair clung to her neck, and bloody sores oozed down her arms.

The bundle she held looked strange against her robotic movements and vacant gaze.

"Something's not right," I said mostly to myself.

"Oh, don't you worry, darling. The poor infected Walker will be put out of its misery in just a moment. I'm surprised she isn't already dead, she looks to be in the final stages of the disease," Lois pondered aloud.

The Walker continued to trudge closer, and a gnawing feeling in my gut told me to go to her. I placed my hand on the door, and Lois screeched, "Stay inside, you fool!"

I ignored her and opened the door. The air was hot and humid, the air was heavy and smelled like smoke. I slowly made my way towards the Walker. It was as if a magnetic force urged me forward. I was drawn to her, fate *demanded* I give this infected Walker my attention.

"Ash! Don't go any closer!" I heard a familiar voice yell from behind. Huxley. "We don't know if she's violent!" he shouted.

I should have felt fear but felt nothing. A calm washed over me.

"I'm fine, I just need to see something," I yelled over my shoulder while keeping my eyes on the infected Walker. I knew if my eyes connected with

Huxley's, I would lose my nerve and not follow through with my insane plan.

Each step I made felt heavy with tense anticipation. The Walker continued to drag herself down the strip. Not once did she notice me walking towards her. Huxley continued to yell at me, begging me to stop, and I heard the slamming of windows as they opened. I felt the eyes of the entire Providence on me as I made my way towards her.

Once I was finally in front of the infected walker, I noticed scarring hidden behind sores on her face, indicating that she was once a Scavenger. Her black clothes were damp with blood, and I heard a muffled cry from the blankets she held.

Her bloodshot eyes were vacant yet penetrating, and I caught the sliver of relief flash through her expression before she collapsed clumsily to her knees. Blood droplets seeped down her skin, and the dry dirt hungrily accepted her offering. Still, the bundle of blankets remained clutched to her heaving chest.

I knelt so that we were eye level. I timidly reached my hands out towards her and grabbed the wool blanket from her weak arms. Slowly breaking eye contact with the Walker, I studied the bundle in my arms. It was the most beautiful baby I had ever seen. White hair framed its plump cheeks. Its heart-shaped lips were cracked, indicating dehydration. The baby appeared to be only a few months old, and I thanked whatever god that was watching that I had listened to my gut.

I peered back up at the infected Walker who was wavering where she sat. I saw the hint of a smile grace her busted and bloody lips before she coughed; blood splattered all over the baby and me.

"Ash, please move," Huxley pleaded in a sad voice. I looked back at him and saw that he had his arrow aimed and ready. The reality of my situation made a stabbing grief prickle beneath my skin.

Once again, I looked at the Walker woman. She was in the final stages of her disease and should have easily died days ago. Her strength and resolve spoke volumes about her love for the child in my arms. I wanted to remember everything about this profound woman that, against all odds, did everything she could for her child.

I nodded an unspoken promise to the Walker woman, one that said I would care for her child, and that it was okay to let go. It was okay to cross the threshold into peace, knowing that her baby was cared for.

I stood while carrying the baby, and made my

way back down the street and towards the Clinic where Maverick was. As I passed Huxley while holding the baby, I saw him grimace. We exchanged a wordless exchange full of pain and promise.

Just before I entered the Clinic, I heard the sound of a blade slicing through the air and a thick guttural groan as it hit its intended target. I clutched the baby tighter as it let out a heartbreaking whimper.

Maverick was ready for me when I opened the door, wearing a devastated expression.

"Bring the baby back here. I'll get an IV ready, and we can run some blood tests to check for immunity," he said in a solemn tone.

I knew that the odds of this baby surviving were slim to none, but I was determined to do whatever I could to care for it. The infected Walker woman defied all odds and delivered the baby safely to Dormas. I was going to fulfill her unspoken wishes.

Huxley joined us shortly after Maverick hooked the baby up to a monitor and got an IV set up. It would take an hour to determine if the baby was immune or not, and once we knew, we could make decisions on what to do next. I stared at the sleeping baby with wonder while pleading with God that she was immune like me. The alternative would be devastating.

"I didn't see the baby. I could have killed him," Hux murmured.

"Her," I interjected. "It's a girl." I wondered what her name was.

"Ah, Ashleigh. The tests are running as we speak," Maverick began. He exchanged a cautionary look with Huxley. "But I just want you to prepare yourself . . ."

I wasn't ignorant of the facts. I knew the survival rates. I was well aware of the percentages of immune individuals. It was a narrative I'd been told my whole life. I knew that this sad story wasn't over, not by a long shot.

"I know, Maverick. Can we just pretend the baby's going to be okay for a little while?" I asked.

Huxley gripped the counter and stared at me with the eyes of someone that has seen too much.

"Let me know," he croaked out before leaving, his head hung low. Eventually, Huxley and I would have to discuss what happened, but not now.

I played with the baby's hair while she slept to the sound of the heart monitor's beeping. She looked worn but so incredibly peaceful. I felt an inexplicable connection to this child. I, too, was orphaned by a disease that stole life without rhyme or reason. But unlike me, I was determined for this child to have a different story.

The hour passed painfully slow, but finally, Maverick's stoic form appeared in the room. The frown on his face made my stomach plummet.

"I have good news, and I have bad news," he began. I clutched my stomach in preparation.

"She is not immune, but it looks like X hasn't attached itself to her platelets yet. If I give her the vaccine now, it *could* prevent her from getting sick," he said while peering at her. "I still want to keep her for observation. Sometimes the vaccine can be tricky in younger children, and I want to double and triple check that she is not infected."

"But she'll be okay?" I asked, unwilling to feel too hopeful.

"I think she'll be okay." He nodded while administering the vaccine in her IV.

I clung to the little victory and gently held the baby's hand.

"Let's call her Hope."

CHAPTER FOURTEEN

Hope cried constantly. During our week at the Clinic together, I rocked her, fed her, changed her diaper, and walked the floors while bouncing her. She only slept when exhaustion claimed her, but even then, it was a short-lived relief from her cries.

It broke my heart. I knew that on a primal level, she craved her mother. She was grieving the loss of someone she barely got the opportunity to know. In turn, it put me in a solemn mood. I felt the pull of sadness while thinking how unfair it all was. Hope and I fed off each other's melancholy and wallowed in our combined grief.

Kemper brought by his old baby crib—hand crafted by his grandfather. He tried to soothe her, but she still screamed. Maverick did numerous checks to ensure that everything was okay, and he found nothing wrong. The vaccine seamlessly did its job preventing X from killing her after being exposed to her mother. Her survival and story were extraordinary.

Cyler stopped by a couple times but was terrified to hold her. He watched with sad eyes from across the room as I tried to soothe her. Jacob was stuck at the train station but called regularly. Patrick brought me clothes to change into—clothes that were a bit too tight, I might add—but he didn't stay long once Hope's shrill cries started back up.

Huxley never did come back. When Maverick called him to say that Hope would be okay, Hux had simply said "Good" before hanging up his tablet.

My nights with Hope in the Clinic completely eradicated my reservations. It was on the third day, that I realized I had been in the Clinic without feeling haunted by all that happened there. The rooms no longer felt like the echo of the Walker woman that died there. Instead, it felt like Hope.

On my seventh day, Maverick determined that she was safe enough to get off observation and suggested that we move back to the manor. While I packed up my clothes and cleaned the room, Mia walked in, covering her ears to block out Hope's poor wails. I waved but didn't bother greeting her. She wouldn't have heard me anyway.

Mia bent over the wooden cradle and picked up Hope, then held her out away from her body as if the baby was a monster and she needed to keep her as far away as possible.

"She sure is loud for such a little body," she observed while tilting her head to the side. Hope stopped crying and furrowed her thin eyebrows at Mia as if trying to understand what was happening. They stared at each other for a moment, until Hope began crying again. I checked the clock and determined that it was time to attempt another feeding. After warming the bottle, I picked her up, and she greedily started sucking down the milk. I sighed in relief.

"So, what's the plan with her?" Mia asked while staring at me in pity. I'm sure I looked terrible. Puke ran down my dress, and my hair was in knots.

"I'm not sure. A woman and her three husbands stopped by yesterday," I began while thinking back to our meeting. The woman was sweet, and her husbands absolutely adored her. I wanted to pick her mind and see how the dynamic of their relationship worked, but they were there for Hope. "Hope cried the entire time, so they didn't bond." I desperately wanted Hope to be loved .

"Well, I stopped by because I know a couple that would be absolutely *perfect* for Hope, and I'm not just saying that because it's my cousin and his husband." She smiled while gauging my expression to see my reaction. "Of course, if you were planning on adopting her as your own, you can forget I said anything," she quickly added.

I looked down at Hope and wondered what our lives would be like if I kept her with me. I knew that my new family would support us, but the idea of being a single mom in this crazy world was nerve-wracking. Besides, I felt too *broken* . I didn't know if I was what Hope needed. I was still grieving my own upbringing, how could I focus on hers?

"I don't think I'm what's best for Hope right now," I whispered, feeling selfish and self-centered. "I want to be in her life, but I think she deserves better."

Hope had given up on the bottle and was starting to sleep. She gripped one of my long curls and yanked it; it was one of her favorite soothing mechanisms for drifting off into a peaceful nap.

"I think you're right." Mia shrugged. I appreciated her brash nature. "I know that you're the type to feel obligated to care for her. I also think you'd give her a good life, but there are people out there that would love her just as much, minus the guilt and resentment. She needs a family, not a hero." Mia plopped one of her dainty hands on my shoulders. Her words stung a little, but she was right. I wanted to love Hope's place in my life, not resent her.

"Tell me about your cousin," I said.

"Why don't you come with me to the Scavenger village and meet him? See how he, his husband, and Hope get along first before bringing it up. I don't want to get his hopes up if you decide that she should go elsewhere."

"Okay, I'll meet them," I replied just as Hope spit up on me. I sighed.

We packed up Hope's belongings, and I messaged all the guys on my tablet, telling them where Mia and I were going. Huxley immediately replied .

I'll go with you.

I was shocked that he replied, let alone offered to accompany me.

I changed Hope's clothes and cleaned up the last of the Clinic before Huxley arrived with Jacob. They both greeted Mia with short hugs before peering at me.

"You ready?" Jacob asked. I think he sensed my conflicted feelings the most.

"Let's do this."

To save us the walk, Huxley borrowed the community transport, and we were at the Scavenger village within a half hour. I was amazed by how quickly they had set up camp on the outskirts of Dormas and was happy to once again see their orange tents and playful children.

With sure steps, Mia led us to one of the tents. Hope wriggled in my arms with such force that on two occasions she almost fled from my arms.

"You got her?" Jacob asked with a smile.

"At least she's not crying," I replied with a shrug.

Mia whistled at a tent's entrance, and after a brief pause, the door flap opened, revealing a very muscular man that looked to be even taller than Hux. He had blue tattoos in tribal designs all down his arms and a blue stripe in his shoulder-length white hair.

"Bowden! Mia's here!" he yelled while hunching over to open the flap of the tent wider and exiting the tent. He was *definitely* taller than Huxley. "And she's brought some guests!"

Soon, a slightly shorter but still impressive man also emerged from the tent. He had short white hair and piercing blue eyes. The designs on his arm were also blue.

"Mia!" the shorter man, who I assumed was Bowden, exclaimed. "What do we owe the pleasure? And you brought a *baby!*" he practically squealed. His deep voice went up an octave once he saw Hope wriggling in my tired arms.

"Bowden, Thurst, these are my friends," Mia said while gesturing to us. "I was visiting with them and wanted to introduce you all. Besides, I know how much you love babies." She smiled brightly at them.

The taller man, Thurst, bent over and looked at Hope with intense eyes. I waited for the inevitable wails to erupt from her tiny frame, but none came. Instead, she held out her hands for him to hold her.

"May I?" he asked.

"Of course," I replied in a shaky voice. I was equal parts jealous and shocked by her immediate acceptance of him.

Huxley stood watch over all of us without saying a word, but Jacob quickly scrounged up some wood and got a fire roaring in the pit outside their tent. We all sat on benches as Thurst and Bowden took turns playing with Hope.

Bowden and Thurst complemented each other

well, it was almost like they could speak telepathically. They moved in unison and anticipated each other's needs.

"How did you two meet?" I asked. I wanted to know more about their relationship, and if there was room for Hope in their family.

"I was exiled from my tribe. My brother won the leadership trials and decided I was too much of a threat to his position," Thurst told me as Bowden grabbed his hand. "I never wanted to lead our tribe, but I couldn't argue. I traveled here because I heard rumors that they were accepting new members if they could fight"

"Naturally," Mia interrupted, "our old Chief had him compete against our best warrior, which at the time was Bowden."

"At the time? I might be a bit older, but I can still kick your ass, Mia," Bowden joked.

"It was the best fight I've ever seen! They were exact equals. Every movement. Every punch. It was incredible," Mia said dreamily.

"Chief declared us both winners. And naturally, I gallantly offered to tend to Thurst's injuries, because I'm selfless like that," he said with a wink .

"I remember that. You sure took a long time in the medic tent," Mia said with an eye roll.

"We've been together ever since," said Bowden with a grin.

"Complete equals," Thurst added.

I watched as they smiled at one another then directed their attention back to Hope. Bowden fed Hope with one of the bottles I brought as Thurst lovingly ran his fingers over her soft hair.

"Can I get you anything to eat?" Bowden asked while cooing at Hope. She soaked up his attention like a sponge and giggled back. It was so plain to see that the three of them were meant for each other.

"No, we actually must get back to Dormas soon," I said with a sigh. The sleepless nights from the past week were wearing me down, and it felt like anvils were on my eyelids. I noticed Thurst and Bowden's shoulders slump. They were truly enjoying their time with Hope.

"You all are welcome to come back anytime, and please bring Hope. You have such a beautiful daughter," Thurst said. He gripped Bowden's knee, and I saw how much they craved a family.

"Actually, I recently rescued Hope. Her mother passed away. We've been searching for a suitable family for her," I said, hoping that they would both catch on to my hint.

Like flashes of lightning they both exchanged quick glances before speaking at once.

"Oh we would simply love— "

"If you are still seeking a family— "

They spoke over one another and started stuttering under the excitement. Hope giggled once again. Bowden placed a firm hand on Thurst's knee and nodded.

"If you are still looking for a family for Hope, we would absolutely love the opportunity. We've been together ten years and think it's time for our family to grow," Thurst said with glistening eyes.

"I think Hope would love that very much," I said with a tentative smile. Bowden leaped from the log he was sitting on and tackled me in a hug .

"Thank you, thank you," he said over and over through happy tears. His sincere joy caused my own eyes to water, and I wondered what my life would have been like had a couple like Bowden and Thurst adopted me.

"I'd still like to be a part of her life, if you'll have me of course," I said shyly. I felt a hand on my shoulder and turned to see Huxley's silent figure looming over me.

"Of course," Thurst immediately replied while happily bouncing Hope on his knee.

We unloaded all of Hope's clothes and gear, minus the crib. I assumed that, one day, Kemper would want his own child to use the cradle his grandfather once carved. Thurst and Bowden said goodbye to us with tears streaming down their faces, and Mia stayed behind to help them get settled.

"That was a good thing you did back there," Jacob said while sliding his hand in mine.

"I did nothing," I replied with a shrug. Huxley began to take large strides ahead of us towards the transport, distancing himself from us as quickly as possible. Jacob noticed Huxley's rough attitude, and after kissing the top of my hand, he ran to the transport and got in before locking the door. He rolled down the windshield just as I walked up to it.

"The two of you need to talk, and I'm not unlocking the door until you do," Jacob said while rolling the window back up. Huxley kicked the door with a growl, causing a dent to form.

"Cyler's going to be mad you dented his transport," I said. I sighed and sat down in the dirt. I didn't have the energy to fight Jacob and his stupid plan. I wore exhaustion like a glove and wanted to get this over with. "Talk so we can go," I added.

"I don't know what you want me to say," Huxley

said with a huff. He crossed his arms over his chest and avoided looking at me.

"Say whatever is going to help you not look at me like I'm the worst thing you've ever seen," I said. "It feels like you're mad at me again." I rubbed my sleepy eyes.

"I'm not mad at you." He plopped down in the dirt beside me. "I'm mad at myself. I'm mad that my impulsiveness almost killed someone." He threw a pebble off into the distance. I wondered if Jacob was listening.

"You were just doing what you've always done. You were protecting your community," I said, trying to convince him that it wasn't his fault. It was this crazy world we lived in. A world where we had to kill first, ask questions later. A single tear fell down my face, but I was too tired to wipe it away. Huxley turned his head and peered at me.

"If you weren't there, Hope would have died," he said. I felt empathetic towards all that plagued Huxley. "I would have released that fucking arrow and . . ." His voice trailed off into nothing, but I knew what he struggled to say.

"I couldn't have done what you did either. It takes both sides of the coin, Hux." The suffering Walker woman's bloody face, and the sound of the arrow hitting her chest, pierced my mind as more tears fell.

"It's all so fucked up." He pulled a flask from his pants and took two large gulps. I heard the transport's door open, and soon Jacob was sitting down beside me, too.

"Agreed," I replied with mock confidence. We sat outside the transport for a while longer in silence. I mourned my parents, Hope's mother, Josiah, and my childhood. I teetered along my breaking point. It felt like I was dancing on the edge of eternity.

I bottled up my scars, and we went back to the Black Manor.

CHAPTER FIFTEEN

I woke up in Cyler's bed. His minty scent filled the air, and I struggled to pull myself out of the fog of tiredness that still clung to me. Sometime around six in the morning, Cyler's bulky frame shimmied under the covers with me. He had worked all night at the mines, and I was comforted by his sleepy, fumbling hands that found me in the dark of the early morning.

It was ten when I finally pulled myself together enough to get out of bed. Cyler was already gone for the day, he slipped away after kissing me on the forehead about an hour ago. I couldn't fathom how he and the others functioned on such little sleep. I endured one week of exhaustion and could barely stand up, how were they defending an entire Providence?

When I walked into the kitchen, I was greeted by the smell of bacon and Jacob's perfect smile. I gently hugged him from behind while he cooked.

"Thanks for last night," I groggily mumbled into his toned back while he flipped the bacon. He smelled like linen and coffee. He started swaying his hips and humming, forcing us to dance as he cooked .

"Huxley will go years without confronting his feelings if you don't force him into a conversation," he replied. The pop of bacon grease hit the back of my hand, and I released him.

"How did you both work through the Jules situation?" I asked timidly. I knew her betrayal and Huxley's erratic fists were still a sore spot for them all.

Jacob tensed when I asked and focused on the food before speaking. "It took a while before I could talk. Maverick rushed me to a neighboring providence to use their healing pod. My jaw and ribs were broken. I don't even want to think about how much it cost him." Jacob absentmindedly rubbed his jaw. "It's hard to think of Huxley as the cause of that."

"During my two weeks in the pod, Huxley went on a bender. He picked fights with the other miners, drank himself stupid, and a few other things he prob-ably wouldn't want me sharing with you."

I imagined Huxley's self-destructive behavior going into overdrive, and the image was painful to think about. I also hated to think of Jacob's wounds. Two weeks in a healing pod meant that he sustained *very* extensive injuries.

"Do you . . ." I trailed off, unsure if I should ask, or if I could handle the answer. "Do you know why Huxley reacted the way he did? It just seems so irra-tional and out of character for him. He's always three steps ahead of the rest of us."

Jacob tensed up and looked at me with devas-tated eyes. "I don't think that's my story to tell, Ash." I nodded in understanding. I wanted to know all the things that tormented them but knew when not to push.

"Anyway," Jacob began again with a frown, "when I finally came to, the guys begged me to find Huxley and bring him back to his senses. I wandered around Dormas until I found him in the mines, drunk off his ass." Jacob let out a light chuckle while turning off the burner and placing bacon, eggs, and toast on a white porcelain plate.

"I knew Huxley was punishing himself. He's self-destructive by nature, so I just did the first thing that came to my mind. I punched him. *Hard.* It hurt me more than it hurt him probably. Poor guy was so drunk he couldn't speak. I knew we couldn't move past this unless I did that. We threw punches while the rest of the guys waited outside. We both ended up leaving the mines bloodied but laughing, and we haven't brought it up since."

"Men are so strange." I sighed while popping a bite of eggs into my mouth.

"No," Jacob began. He thrust out a thumb and wiped food from the corner of my lips. "*Huxley* is strange. I was more than happy to talk about my feelings and hold hands, or whatever it is normal people do, but that's not what Huxley *needed* . He needed to feel like things were even between us. He needed someone to kick his ass. Even though punching him damn near broke my hand, I gave that to him because our friendship meant more to me than my anger."

I watched Jacob with a slightly broader sense of understanding. Their group was his whole life. They meant more to him than his pain, his grief, and his anger.

"Did you ever allow yourself to feel angry, Jacob?" I asked. Jacob seemed to push down all his emotions, an impulse I could relate to lately.

"Of course. But I was more motivated by the fear

of losing the only family I've ever known," Jacob said while pushing away a completely cleared plate. He ate his breakfast fast and was happily leaning back in his chair despite the dark mood of our conversation.

"Everyone called her Momma Black—Cy's Mom. She was just this extremely nurturing and self-less woman. Momma Black found me when I was four years old at the Train station. I—I don't remember much before that," Jacob said while looking at his hands. "I have these vague memories of my birth mom sneaking me onto a train to Dormas. I think she hoped I'd have better luck here than in the Zone. Momma Black took me in. Raised me like her own. Loved me until her death."

I wished in that moment, that I could have met Momma Black. I desperately wanted to know the woman that shaped such strong and caring men.

"Cy, Maverick, Hux, Patrick, Kemper, and even Jules are the only family I've ever known. I'd do anything to preserve that," Jacob said. I noticed his eyes shimmering with emotion, and I tried not to feel jealous that Jules was included in that. *I* wanted to be his family.

But I knew that regardless of the vicious tendrils of jealousy, that this was a tight knit group. Even Jules had her place in their family dynamic, no matter how bratty she was. They were brought together by sadness and loss. Bonded by resilience.

"You're a part of that too, Ash," Jacob whispered before kissing my forehead. He grabbed my hands and pulled me up before guiding me towards the kitchen counter.

"The moment I saw you, I knew you were special," he whispered while pushing me with his hips against the counter. My nightgown shimmied up, revealing more of my thighs and I bent my knee so that it was between Jacob's legs.

"You feel it too, don't you?" He reached behind me to grab a coffee cup and take a sip. He placed the cup back down on the granite countertop, and framed my body with his strong arms, locking me into his intense stare.

"Feel what?" I asked in a low tone. Each breath caused my chest to brush against his in teasingly slow strides. My nipples pebbled at the contact, and I cursed my thin nightgown.

"You feel like we're on the cusp of something amazing. Like we're all just waiting for someone to jump," he whispered. I watched how his perfect and plump lips popped on the last word. I wanted to kiss him. I wanted to know what it felt like to fall and be caught.

"Cy wanted you to visit the new school house," he said before walking towards the sink. He started washing the dirty dishes. "I told him and Kemper you'd be by in a little bit. Wear your painting dress," he said with a wink before walking away.

The school house was conveniently located near the General Store in the community center, so it was a fairly short walk. Originally, they had planned to turn the Walker Dorms into a school house, but suggested a building more centrally located, and Cyler readily agreed. The sun beat down on my bare, freckled shoulders. I wore my tan sleeveless dress with convenient pockets and an overabundance of paint splatters, displaying the many different projects I've worked on since moving to Dormas.

The school house was a small wooden building with a curved roof and porch. I heard the sound of hammers clanging and followed the noise inside where I found Cyler, Patrick, and Kemper installing a thin, clear screen. Cyler had made arrangements for some of the best scholars in the empire to telecommute in for lessons.

The ceilings were tall, and six clear tables with

white chairs were scattered around the room. Various stations with supplies and experiments littered the outer corners of the room.

"Ah! Just in time!" Kemper exclaimed once he saw me, causing him to accidentally release his hold on the screen. Cyler and Patrick loudly cursed as it slipped, and all of them frantically caught the screen before repositioning it in place and screwing it into the wall. I noticed Kemper blush a deep shade of red in embarrassment.

"Hey, babe, I hope you don't mind, but I'm putting you to work today," Cyler said in an animated tone as he beamed proudly around the room. He was excited.

"Jacob told me to wear my painting dress . . .?" I looked around at the white walls and wondered where to start.

"We have a *very* important painting job for you. It'll be the highlight of your artistic career!" Patrick joked just as the white door burst open and about two dozen excited kids ran through the entrance of the school house. I laughed at their carefree nature as they jumped on tables and explored every inch of the classroom.

"We want—" Cyler began before scolding a little

boy. "No climbing on the desks!!" The boy leaped onto the floor and began running in circles .

Cyler picked up another girl that was climbing and threw her over his massive shoulders while a little boy clung to his leg. He walked over to me while carrying both of them.

"We want to put their handprints on that wall," he explained while setting them down with a chuckle and running over to another child that was putting smudgy handprints on the screen just installed.

I laughed as the guys chased kids around the small school house. Each of them seemed wildly out of their element, and I was amused by their frantic expressions. However, my mood turned sour when I saw Jules stroll through the front door in her usual stuffy manner.

"What are you doing here?" I asked with an exasperated sigh. I wasn't in the mood for her rudeness.

"Not that it's any of *your* business," she began in her usual condescending and hostile attitude, "but my mother was once the school teacher for Dormas. I —I volunteered to bring the kids here," she concluded in a slightly lower and wistful tone. I watched as she admired the school building with a slight smile. It suddenly became clear to me why this school house was so important to Cyler, it was for Momma Black.

Likewise, this was important to Jules. I understood the look of awe on her face as her eyes inspected each corner of the room proudly— it was the same look I had while painting or baking. Her thin lips even quirked up in a half smile as Cyler showed a little girl how to use some blocks.

"I truly do hope he finds a good school teacher. I know he's hired scholars to video in, but he'll need someone here full time." She gave me a scrutinizing glare. "I'm the only one in Dormas with a decent education, they can't just let *anyone* off the streets mold the minds of our next generation." Jules puffed out her chest in indignation and flexed her thin fingers at her side.

My Walker upbringing only allowed for a basic education mostly focused around cooking, cleaning, and proper etiquette. I found myself jealous of Jules. I wished I knew more about the world and fleetingly wondered if Cyler would let me sit in on a few classes.

"If I weren't forced to work in the gardens, I would be a sure-win for the job. I've had the best tutors in the entire Empire," she added with a frown.

"Aren't you a bit young to be a school teacher?" I

asked. Sometimes I forgot that she was just sixteen, almost seventeen. Jules was far too jaded for someone her age. She turned her head and peered at me, as if just now realizing that we were talking.

"I wasn't *too* young to be married off to a stranger and moved across the empire to another Providence. Besides, I'll be seventeen in three months," she replied with angst.

"I suppose you're right," I gave her a sideways glance. "Perhaps you'd make a good school teacher, Jules."

Luckily, a loud screech from a little girl with blonde, curly ringlets relieved us from having to talk further. Jules immediately took charge.

"Children, settle down this instant!" she yelled, her shrill voice echoing across the room. Immediately, twenty-six pairs of wide eyes were on her. Unsurprisingly, she completely commanded their attention. "Find a seat and sit down quietly. I don't want to hear any chatter," she ordered with a smirk.

Kemper set up paint tins while Patrick explained what to do. The kids squirmed in their seats, and occasionally Jules coughed, reminding them that she was there and watching. She made an excellent rule-enforcer.

We made quick work of applying paint to the

children's hands and placing them on the back wall. A wide variety of prints and colors filled the space in a colorful array. After six spills, two meltdowns, and about four hundred stern looks from Jules, the children left—after Jules left with an indignant huff of dissatisfaction, of course. We simply couldn't have one interaction that didn't end in needless hostility .

I started to clean up, but Kemper clicked his tongue and grabbed the paint pan from me.

"Not so fast," he said. He grabbed a brush and began painting my hand a beautiful shade of lilac. Each swipe of the paintbrush sent tingles up my arm, and I watched as he took extra care to slowly cover my skin. Once he felt thoroughly done, he took my hand and gently placed it on the wall. We both stood there close to one another for longer than necessary. My hand burned where he touched me, and he observed me with a half-smile.

"We needed your handprint to make it complete," he said shyly while looking at me. I peered up at him through my lashes, and he took a step closer. "Ash, I— "

Cyler loudly cursed, startling us. I jumped and accidentally placed my lilac covered hand on Kemper's white shirt over his chest.

We both giggled, then turned to see the cause of

Cyler's outburst. Someone had dipped the ends of his black hair in pink paint. We roared laughing at the look of him as he began frantically picking off the spots that were dried and flaky.

"Damn kids!" Cyler exclaimed.

Patrick snapped a couple pictures before Cyler tackled him for his tablet, causing more paint to fly. It would be a long night of cleaning. I simply looked at Kemper and his now ruined shirt and giggled.

"Sorry I ruined your shirt," I said apologetically as Kemper dusted himself off and walked back over to me. I wanted to ask him what it was he was going to say before Cyler interrupted us, but the moment had gone.

"Nonsense." Kemp looked lovingly at his no longer perfect, crisp white shirt. "You made it better."

CHAPTER SIXTEEN

Patrick's mischievous laughter filtered throughout the General Store. It took another day to fully recuperate from the emotional and physical toll that saving Hope took on my body. I felt a gnawing uncertainty about Lois and Mark. Their nonchalant views on the infected Walker Woman made me cringe in discomfort. However, I was happy to be back within the familiarity of the Bakery and once again doing what I enjoyed.

Patrick was visiting today. He and Huxley ordered pastries for the mine workers every couple of weeks, and today he stopped by a bit early so we could chat while I prepared his order. He sat at the wooden counter on a stool while I iced some of the pastries. He gossiped about some of the workers and shared some of his more recent shenanigans.

". . . and just the other day we hid Huxley's desk deep within the mines. He was *furious* . He thought it was the other mine workers, but it was me." He chuckled in amusement, and I shook my head in mock discontent. I liked that Patrick was playful and silly. "Damn thing was heavy as hell, but it was worth it to see him get mad."

"I *knew* it was you that moved my desk," a familiar angry voice filled the air. I turned to see Huxley walking up to the Bakery counter in heavy strides. He pulled up a seat, and just before sitting down, yanked Patrick's chair out from underneath him, causing Patrick to crash rather ungracefully to the floor. Huxley smiled as he sat, then wiped his expression clean once he saw me looking.

"What are you doing here?" Patrick asked. He dusted himself off with a knowing smirk as I started making a new batch of cream cheese icing.

"I figured you could use some help carrying it all to the Mines," Huxley hurriedly explained, tensing up. Patrick raised an eyebrow but didn't question him further. I refused to think that it was because he *wanted* to spend time with me. Wishful thinking was for the hopeless.

I started to mix together my ingredients and the twins watched in fascination. "If you're good, I'll let you lick the spoon," I said with a surprisingly coy smile, but Huxley merely coughed while Patrick licked his lips. I realized how flirtatious I sounded and blushed. I shook off the brief embarrassment and continued mixing the icing, while their identical eyes followed every movement I made. Once it was the consistency I liked, I put it in a funnel and began drizzling it onto the pastries.

"Oh, Ash! I wanted to introduce you to a couple of my friends!" Lois' weak voice yelled throughout the store. I sighed in frustration. Lois was back to introducing me to new suitors.

"Help me!" I whispered frantically to the guys while wiping my hands on my apron. Lois was determined to marry me off, and each suitor got progressively worse. How could I look at another when already I had six *very* handsome men that occupied my every waking thought?

"What's wrong, Ash? Not a people person?" Patrick joked.

"I'm just tired of being introduced to five new suitors every day," I forced out in a whisper. "I thought she would have run out of men by now." I groaned. Patrick and Huxley suddenly went rigid .

"How long has this been going on?" Huxley asked as Lois rounded the corner with two men trailing behind her.

"Since I started working here." I forced a fake smile into place.

"Have you been, uh, courted by anyone?" Huxley asked awkwardly, but Lois pushed between Huxley and Patrick's chairs and smiled at me before I could respond.

"Oh, darling, look at you. Always baking! She makes my shop smell so wonderful," Lois said with a grin while speaking to two men that followed behind her. They were handsome but didn't make my stomach flutter with anticipation.

"This is Norman and Peter." As Lois introduced them, she held her arm out in a clumsy misplaced bow that made me flush hot with awkward embarrassment.

Norman had blond hair and a crooked smile. His thick muscles were hidden beneath a baggy emerald shirt. Black residue clung to the skin on the tips of his fingers, hinting that he worked in the mines. Peter was thin with dark hair and wide eyes. He had two dimples and a mischievous grin.

"Hello, Norman and Peter, are you here to order something?" I asked, my tone forced and polite.

Huxley clutched the edge of the countertop, while Patrick looked at me with mild amusement.

"Well, we're actually here to call upon you, Mistress. We've heard all about your beauty from Mistress Caverly, but I must say, my hopes and dreams were but a hazy prayer compared to your natural glow," Peter said with a bow.

Norman cringed in embarrassment. They seemed to be complete opposites, and yet they were *both* calling on me. *Together.* When in Dormas, I guess.

"I'm so sorry to break it to you, Peter, but Ashleigh is spoken for," Patrick said while getting off his stool. He walked around the counter and wrapped a thick arm around me.

I dropped my mouth open in surprise. Ever the opportunist, Patrick saw my opened mouth and swooped up a dollop of icing before plopping it onto my tongue. I closed my lips over his finger and licked up the sugary thick icing in a bold reflex that reminded me of the night of our almost-kiss on my birthday.

Lois emitted a shrill squeal of excitement. I watched as her fingers twitched at her side. She itched to grab her tablet and call everyone within a thirty-mile radius to gossip about this new revelation.

"Oh my! Please forgive me, Patrick, I assumed your relationship was more of a friendly nature. I didn't realize she was in a courtship with anyone, is it just you? Or...?" she asked while peering at Huxley.

"That's because we've been keeping it quiet. Ashleigh is very shy, aren't you sweetheart?" Patrick asked while squeezing my hip.

"Ye-Yes." The room suddenly felt very hot, and I felt Huxley's exasperated stare on me and Patrick.

"And by 'we' you mean . . .?" Lois dug further. She seemed determined to be the first to crack open the juicy gossip and share with anyone that listened. Norman and Peter looked wildly uncomfortable. I noticed them shuffling farther and farther away from my counter.

"By 'we' I mean the entire Dormas Leadership Council," Patrick said with a serious face. Once again, I was shocked. I opened my mouth to disagree; Patrick didn't need to lie to these people. I was more than capable of letting these men down on my own.

"Actually—" I began.

"Actually, Ash was just going to help us deliver these pastries to the mine," Huxley jumped in while standing up. He walked over to my would-be suitors and shook their hands with much more force than necessary, causing Norman and Peter to frantically excuse themselves. Their whispered fighting was heard as they left the store. I quickly iced and boxed up the remaining pastries, then fled Lois' questioning stare with Huxley and Patrick.

Once out of earshot, I yelled at Patrick. "What on earth was that?!" I scolded. Patrick was walking backwards, facing me and Huxley. He didn't even have the decency to look ashamed, if anything, he appeared *pleased* .

"Whatever do you mean?" Patrick asked. He looked way too proud of himself. Huxley simply grumbled under his breath and pounded the ground with his feet.

"I mean," I began. "Telling Lois and those guys that I—I'm, uh, *courting* all of you," I said with much less steam than before. I felt an embarrassing flush cover my cheeks, and if I weren't holding boxes of pastries, I might have covered my face with my hands. I found it so strange that, already, this was an idea I found appealing.

"Ah. Yes, well, I've learned that in order for something to come to fruition, one must face their desires head on." Patrick gave me a wink as he turned around and got in step with us.

"What does that even mean?" I asked incredulously.

"It means," Huxley began, "that my brother is a presumptuous dick."

I chuckled as Patrick debated on dropping his box of pastries and punching Hux. "It means, that whatever happens, happens," Patrick said, causing Hux to growl again.

"I thought I was supposed to treat you all like my brothers—" I began.

"Oh yuck, yeah . . . well let's nip that one in the bud right now," Patrick interrupted while wearing a firmly set look of pure disgust. "Regardless of whatever happens, please, for the love of all that is holy, don't ever, *ever* refer to me as your brother again." Patrick gave an exaggerated shiver.

"Uh, I second that one," Huxley added sheepishly.

"You do realize that Lois probably has sent out a mass newsletter to everyone by now. They'll be planning our wedding within the week!" I exclaimed. Patrick gave me a sideways glance and bit his lip.

"You'd look good in red," Patrick whispered.

"Red?"

"It's tradition for brides to wear red," he replied.

"Can we *please* talk about something else?" Huxley begged. "Look, just ignore them, we did you a favor. Now Lois will stop bringing suitors to the

Bakery, and you can go about your day. We know the truth, and that's all that matters. None of us are fucking courting you," Huxley said with such conviction that each beat of my heart felt like the crunching gravel beneath his feet. It was nice to pretend that this was a reality; that I could have all of them, but once again, Huxley doused me in an ice cold bucket of reality.

"Well, look who's being the dick now," Patrick said to Huxley while rolling his eyes and taking my box of treats and piling it on top of his. "Go on back to the Bakery, sweetie, I'll see you tonight," Patrick told me. He somehow managed to juggle the three boxes he was carrying and kiss my cheek.

Before leaving, I decided to make it known that I could have handled the situation without their help. "For the record," I began with a frown. "I didn't *need* your help. Maybe I wanted to get to know Norman and—and...what was his name again?" My anger fizzled out as I tried to remember his name.

Huxley didn't dignify my statement with a response. Instead, he simply stomped off like he usually did when he was feeling particularly moody. Once Huxley was out of sight, Patrick placed the boxes on the dirt ground and stormed towards me.

"For the record," Patrick said while grabbing my

face in his hands. He had a determined, steely look in his eyes. "This courtship between you and me? It's real," he said before placing a firm, chaste kiss upon my lips. I wanted to linger in the sensation, but he pulled away, picked up his food, and followed after Huxley.

CHAPTER SEVENTEEN

Cyler called a Leadership Council meeting the next day. He insisted I attend and make his favorite dinner. For the first time since my birthday, Cyler, Huxley, Patrick, Maverick, Jacob, and Kemper were all in the same place at the same time, and I was giddy with excitement. Although I craved one on one time with each of them, I couldn't help but feel drawn to their group. Together they were vibrant and full of life. They brought out the best in each other, the best in *me*.

Cyler watched me cook from his perch at the dinner table while he occasionally typed on his tablet. We were waiting for the others to arrive—as always, they were working up until the last possible minute.

"What's the meeting about tonight, Cy?" I asked while putting my casserole dish in the oven.

Cyler looked up at me and gave me a forced smile while turning off his tablet and setting it down. "I'd prefer to wait and discuss it whenever we're all together, babe," he replied.

I couldn't help but slump my shoulders at this. The last time Cyler 'surprised' me with something, it was Jules' and Josiah's engagement.

"Should I be worried?" I asked, still feeling persistent.

"I don't *think* so," was all Cyler said in response. His assurance fell flat, and I grumbled at his inability to just spit it out.

One by one, each of the others began to arrive. Jacob greeted me with a flirty smile and a kiss on the cheek before dipping his finger in the homemade ice-cream I made this morning.

"What did we even eat before you came along?" he mused while swiping another finger-full and walking upstairs to shower before the dinner meeting.

Patrick and Huxley arrived next. Huxley greeted me with a nod and a small grin, which was more than he usually graced me with these days, and in usual

Patrick fashion, I was plucked from the stove and spun around while he sang silly nursery rhymes. A few days ago, I casually mentioned that I never learned any during my childhood in the Stonewell home, and Patrick was now making it his mission to make sure I learned each and every song imaginable.

"Ring around the rosey, a pocket full of poseys. Ashes, Ashes, we all fall down!" he sang while he tickled me. I giggled while his fingers moved mercilessly against the sensitive sides of my stomach.

"Again with the nursery rhymes, I see," Maverick said with a smirk, dropping stacks of papers onto the kitchen table. He was researching a new lead on the vaccine and it was keeping him up all hours of the night. He looked exhausted, but his spirit seemed renewed with the possibility of a breakthrough, so I didn't scold him—too much.

"No work at the dinner table, Maverick," I said. I removed myself from Patrick's arms and made my way over to Maverick. Once close enough, he swept a curly strand behind my ear and kissed me on the forehead. Over the last week it had become his standard form of greeting, and I found myself craving his hellos throughout the day.

"How was your day?" I asked. Looking him over,

I saw the black circles under his eyes, but a bright light flashed between his irises that brought joy to his tired face.

Maverick pulled me in for a hug and mumbled into my hair. "I'm so, so close, Ash."

Cyler's rough voice broke us apart. "Stop distracting the chef! She's got a very important job to do, you know!" he joked while trying to sneak a bite of some left over cake I brought home from the Bakery. I walked towards him and playfully slapped his wrist before going back to work while Cyler and Maverick discussed an issue between the mine workers and the new Scavengers.

Kemper arrived just as I was finishing up dinner. I looked up to greet him with a smile, but instead of his usual happy stare, I was greeted with a look of utter terror. I stopped chopping vegetables for the salad and went to him.

"Kemper, what's wrong? You look terrible."

His eyes scanned the room and everyone became silent. I noticed how the room grew tense, as if preparing for the worst. Every scenario imaginable flashed in my mind, and I reached out to clutch his hand in anticipation.

"Lately, a few of the female Walkers have become a *little* more forward," he began with a shudder. Patrick snorted, and the room erupted into merciless laughter.

"Another naked girl in your office again, Kemp?" Patrick asked, laughing. My eyes snapped to Patrick to gauge the truthfulness of his statement. Surely he was joking?

"No . . . worse. Much, much worse," Kemper replied while pouring himself a glass of whiskey and downing it whole. "I was accosted while trying to use the restroom." He threw up his hands in exasperation. "Becca is relentless!"

The sane part of me wanted to have empathy for Kemper; he was, after all, someone I cared deeply for. But the primal version, the one that felt wildly protective of him, wanted to claw Becca's eyes out. She might be nice, but Kemper was mi— .

"Ash? You okay? You're gripping the end of the table like it bit you," Patrick asked in a concerned voice while licking his bottom lip. I looked down to see that I did, in fact, have a death grip on the mahogany table.

"I'm fine, just concerned for Kemper," I managed to bite out while releasing my hold. Kemper's knowing eyes met mine, and he smiled like he knew what I was thinking and was *pleased* by it.

"I'm just not used to the attention. We haven't

had women in Dormas for a while. I'm going to start telling them that I'm courting someone." Kemper shifted his gaze to me.

"Oh! Haven't you heard? We're all courting Ashleigh," Patrick said while studying his nails nonchalantly.

"What?" Maverick asked immediately while looking at me with the hint of a smile.

"Lois kept tossing some pretty *un* suitable suitors Ash's way. It was pretty pathetic, really. Therefore, being the selfless and benevolent person that I am, I offered myself up, and you all, as her devoted suitors!" Patrick said with a clap of his hands.

"Perfect. I'll add this topic to the Agenda for our Council meeting. We have a few logistics to work out." Cyler grinned, and I remembered our moment in the treehouse.

"We're not fucking taking *minutes* to discuss courting a girl," Huxley said while sucking in a deep breath of air. "I mean, we aren't even courting her, not really."

"Actually, I'll have to agree with Huxley on this one," I said before grinding my teeth in frustration. "None of you have *asked* to court me. Besides, we have much more important matters to discuss. Let's just drop it, please," I begged.

"You didn't even ask her?" Jacob yelled while throwing his hands up. "We are totally fucking this up . . . . A woman should be wooed!"

They each began talking over one another. Huxley glared at me like this was *my* fault. Like I was chaos incarnate, here to ruin him and his family.

Cyler broke the tense discussions going on around me. "Enough! We can talk about all of this later. Let's eat in the meeting room tonight."

I was thankful that he promptly changed the subject. On one hand I wanted definite answers, I wanted to know what it was we were all doing. However, there was a darker part within me that didn't want to deal with my insecurities. I didn't want to face rejection, or worse, complete exclusion from their family.

We all gathered in the meeting room, and to my surprise, Tallis joined us. Luckily, I tend to cook more than necessary, so I had enough to spare. He looked just as wild and exotic as I remembered, but he lacked the bleeding authority he showed in our last meeting.

"Hello, *Agrio*," he said with a smile. He sat down in the chair next to me, patting me on the shoulder. I greeted him back with a friendly smile.

"Ash, would you mind running back into the

kitchen and fetching the mustard seasoning, I find it goes great with this dish," Maverick requested in an even tone, and I happily obliged. Once I had the seasoning and made my way back, I noticed that Jacob had claimed the seat next to Tallis, and there was a newly vacant spot next to Huxley.

Since this was a more formal affair, everyone waited for me to take the first bite, and unlike my first dinner in Dormas, I knew what to expect. I looked around the room with a sly smile as they all stared and slowly, ever so slowly, placed a small bite in my watering mouth. I felt rebellious, but I *enjoyed* feeling their eyes on me, and wanted to revel in their complete attention for as long as possible.

Once I took my bite, a series of scraping utensils and shuffling plates reverberated around the room, and everyone began eating in silent appreciation. I observed Tallis while he ate and noticed that he was watching the others for social cues. When Maverick sipped his drink, so did he. He held his silverware in a clumsy fashion, and I wondered if he usually ate with his hands and not a fork.

"Well, I guess it's time to discuss why I've called you all here," Cyler began while wiping grease from the corners of his mouth with an appreciative smile.

"I've been in communications with the Ethros leaders down south, and they have offered me a deal...one I feel would be foolish to refuse."

"Ugh," Tallis groaned. "Ethros is the armpit of the empire. They have the manners and integrity of an X-infected goat." He snorted and looked around the table, expecting people to laugh at his joke, but none did.

"They have Heat," Cyler said with stoic intensity.

I gasped in shock. Heat was rod-shaped tubes that shot out blasts of concentrated waves of electric fire. One shot turned its victim to ash on impact. Emperor Lackley outlawed them decades ago, but some Providences had underground means of producing them. To be caught trading or making them was punishable by death.

"Absolutely not," Maverick said while standing up. "I've dedicated my existence to the preservation of life, and we decided long ago that we would not involve ourselves in those sorts of trades."

"Let me talk, Mav," Cyler said calmly.

"No, I'm not even entertaining this," Maverick said again. He started walking towards the exit when Tallis interrupted him.

"A wise man hears all sides before passing judgement, Maverick."

Maverick froze and turned back around. He gave Tallis a menacing look that made *my* skin crawl. "There is nothing wise about buying lethal weapons from Ethros," he said with a growl.

"We need better protection," Huxley interrupted. He was scooting his food around his plate and had his blue eyes fixed on a singular spot on the table.

"Whatever, Huxley, I'm right and you know it!" Maverick hollered.

"Being right is subjective. Besides, everyone knows that it's dangerous being right when it's the government that's wrong," Tallis added in a wise voice. "You must greet that danger head on."

Cyler's face grew red, and I sensed that his patience was wearing thin.

"Don't view this as an offensive move," Cyler explained. "It's simply so that we can have an excellent *defense* . A tool that would only be used if we're under attack. I've never been one to seek out opportunities for needless loss of life, Maverick. You of all people should know that."

I watched as their argument grew and opinions

continued to ping pong between everyone, each bounce increasing the tension in the room.

Before I knew it, Cyler and Maverick were yelling at one another while Huxley broke a wooden serving spoon by banging it against the table. Jacob, Kemper, and Patrick watched the madness unfold alongside me.

"I think maybe we should all have the opportunity to voice our concerns or wishes," I suggested in a sure but low voice. This was the first time I'd seen a fight between my makeshift family, and it was jarring to say the least. I stood and made my way over to Maverick, then placed my hand in his, I wanted to show him solidarity and support.

"I think Heat is a very drastic defensive measure, and everyone has a right to feel concerned about the implications of this deal," I began and instantly felt tension leave Maverick's frame. I silently thanked Mistress Stonewell. She was cruel and uncaring, but she taught me how to command a room.

"However," I began, "We must consider the dangers that are upon us. I think that we should look into increasing our defensive measures in the most efficient way possible. It's a hard choice, and I respect Maverick's need to preserve life. I think a vote makes the most sense."

Cyler peered at me, and I saw a millimeter lift in his lips, indicating that he was pleased with my little speech. Every time I asserted myself, his eyes twinkled with satisfaction, and it spurred me further despite the itching self-consciousness that filled me.

"Fine." Maverick sighed while gripping my hand harder. I felt like the anchor keeping him in control.

"Jacob?" I asked. Our eyes connected just before his head dipped and shoulders slumped.

"I'm sorry, Maverick, but Kindle's death could have been prevented. I support having Heat here in Dormas. As long as we approach it with the utmost care," he quickly added.

"Patrick?"

"Against," he replied with a shrug. His lips remained firmly pursed in a straight line. He provided no explanation for his vote, and his eyes shifted around the room as if he was nervous about his opinion and ready for others to judge him for choosing what he did.

"Huxley?"

"For. I'm tired of being the ant hiding from the magnifying glass," he said. I briefly wondered if Huxley *ever* felt like an ant. It seemed implausible that someone so large and intimidating would ever feel so *weak* .

"Kemper?" I asked in a soft voice. I knew he was naturally gentler than the others and could sense I'd predict his answer.

"For. I want to know that I can protect those that I care about," he said while his blue eyes caressed me with such adoration that my cheeks heated. His vote surprised me, but I respected his reasoning.

I looked at Cyler, and he nodded his head yes. I already knew what his answer would be. At the same time, Maverick shook his head no, while scowling deeply at anyone willing to look.

"I'm not sure if my vote counts, but in case anyone cares, I'm against it," Tallis added, surprising me. His earlier comments made it seem that he was supportive of building our arsenal. "I've seen how Heat works. It's a coward's weapon of choice. When I kill, I prefer to use a knife." He pulled out a small dagger and began picking his teeth with the tip of it. "I like to see the whites fade in my enemy's eyes as he dies," he said menacingly with wide, wild eyes that shifted as he spoke, all traces of the wise and gentle leader gone.

"What's your vote, Ash?" Jacob asked with an encouraging half-smile. His hands were folded in front of him, and he anxiously tapped his thumb against the wood of the table.

"I'm not sure my opinion counts, I'm not on the leadership council," I replied while shuffling my feet uncomfortably.

Cyler waved his hand to dismiss my words. "Nonsense. We decided on your birthday that you were on the council," he began. "Maverick, what was the title you gave her? Oh! Yes—Captain of Walker Relations."

I felt a hive of anxiety buzz around my stomach, and I hated everyone just a bit for putting me in this position. I didn't want to hurt anyone with my choice, and I also didn't want to seem like I was taking sides.

I considered my options for a moment while they all held their breath. I felt unqualified to share an opinion, but ultimately, I went with my gut.

"For," I choked out in a whimper. "But as a strictly defensive measure *only* ," I quickly added while avoiding Maverick's tense frame. I knew that my vote was disappointing to him, and I could only hope that he wouldn't push me away.

His hand slipped out of mine. It felt like someone ripping tape off my battered heart. I wanted to run to him and comfort him. I knew his demons were a medley of nightmarish virtues, but I also knew that something would need to happen to defend us against emperorLackley. Nevertheless, his departure left me feeling hollow and guilty.

"Well, I guess it's settled then. I take no joy in causing you pain, brother," Cyler said to Maverick's retreating form.

CHAPTER EIGHTEEN

The next morning, Cyler and Patrick made plans to travel to Ethros at nightfall. A small part of me felt nervous about their trade deal. I couldn't help but feel a nagging sense of unease about it all, regardless of my firm opinion that Dormas was in desperate need of protection. I packed their meals and lingered in both of their rooms while they prepared, soaking up as much time as possible with them.

Cyler was distracted, probably by Maverick's frustration. Patrick, however, sensed my uncertainty and abandoned packing to sing more nursery rhymes and cuddle me on his bed.

"We're going to be fine, Ash. We've been developing good rapport with Ethros for months now."

"Then why can't I come with you?" I asked in a whiny voice that sounded foreign to me. I spent a lifetime in solitude, when did I become so needy?

"Because, someone needs to stay here to keep Huxley from killing anyone, Maverick from sulking in his office, and Jules from cornering Jacob," Patrick said with a chuckle that didn't quite feel authentic enough for the severity of our situation.

"Just be sure to hurry home. I don't think I can handle Huxley's sour attitude without you to buffer it for much more than a week," I said dramatically.

Patrick laughed and moved me so that I was laying on his chest. I felt the rise and fall of each of his breaths and wondered when touching him became such a norm for me. "I promise to come back as soon as I can," he said while nuzzling into my hair. He breathed in my scent, and I felt goosebumps pucker up everywhere his breath touched.

"You guys are the only family I have," I replied.

That night, I hugged both Cyler and Patrick for far longer than socially acceptable. Everyone but Maverick came to see them off, and I fully planned on chastising him for it later, once he was no longer locked in his office avoiding me, of course.

The train mocked me within the confines of the station, and that familiar feeling of dread made my knees shake. Despite our last successful mission in it, I still felt it was bad luck and severely hated that I wouldn't be traveling with them. Now it wasn't just Cyler I had to worry about, it was Patrick, too.

Cyler boldly kissed my cheek so close to my lips that I felt a sliver of a promise between us, as well as a craving for more. Patrick held me tightly against him and kissed the sensitive skin on my neck just below my earlobe, causing quivers to erupt within me. He then sent me a smoldering look that reminded me of our afternoon together. I knew that I would be daydreaming for the days to come about how our bodies were snug and intertwined while we snuggled.

I peered at Patrick and Huxley's goodbye with interest. I wanted to dig deeper into their relationship and see how they handled this dangerous mission. But in a highly anticlimactic move, they simply bumped fists and did an awkward one-handed hug. This was followed by a "see you later" from Patrick. Ugh, men.

During my walk back to the Black Manor, I considered storming up to the Clinic and demanding that Maverick work things out with me, but Jacob kept a firm and wordless grip on my hand, preventing me from making any rash decisions .

"Let's not head home just yet. I wanted to show you something," Jacob said while pulling me towards the trees. My dismal mood immediately brightened at the prospect of spending alone time with Jacob.

"You showing her the spot?" Kemper asked with a grin. The moonlight danced along his blond hair and cast dark shadows along the lines of his face.

"Yeah, you want to come?" Jacob asked unconvincingly.

"Absolutely! It's about time she got a proper initiation. Hux, come on. You've *got* to come with us," Kemper said, clamping his hand upon Huxley's stiff shoulder.

I put my hand behind my neck and looked at their three faces. Jacob looked resigned but still happy, Kemper had pure excitement coursing through his features, and Huxley was *timid* , a word I never thought I'd use to describe him. This 'spot' was important to them.

"Come on, Huxley, you can keep an eye on us," I joked.

He rolled his eyes in such a delicious way that my breath hitched. "Fine. But we can't be out too late, I've got plans with Mia."

With that revelation, my stomach sank—no

—*plummeted*. Why did it affect me so that he was spending time with Mia?

"You make it sound so much more scandalous than it actually is," Jacob said to Huxley while giving my hand a gentle squeeze, as if he could sense that I was disheartened. "You've got guard duty at the same time as her," Jacob explained.

"On the completely opposite side of the Providence," Kemper added. I hated that their explanations made me feel immensely better.

We made our way to the secretive 'spot'. I spent the majority of our walk trying to pry information about it out of them, but all three only provided vague answers and boyish chuckles. As we walked further away from the town, the wildness of the woods made excitement and anticipation course through me. Although I felt safe near Jacob, Kemper, and Huxley, the eeriness of the dark still made me eager to get to our destination .

After tripping over my third stray vine, Jacob gave me a mischievous look before hauling me over his shoulder. I yelped in surprise and felt his hot hands on my thighs, causing my mauve skirt to ride up. "We're about five minutes away, can't have you tripping and scraping that perfect skin of yours before we get there," he said with a laugh.

It was a torturous five minutes. Every step he made, pushed his hand up further, and I loved the feel of it. It made me anxious and tingly all over, and I counted the seconds until he put me back down.

"We're here," he said in a breathless voice while sliding me down his long body and onto the floor of the woods. I placed both my hands against his chest and peered up at him. The moonlight barely illuminated his face, but I saw the flash of his white teeth as he bit his lip.

"Come on, you two," Huxley voice scolded from the dark. I followed the direction of his voice with outstretched hands until I was in a clearing. Leaves crunched under my boots, and the moonlight illuminated the space completely, allowing me to see Kemper, Jacob, and Huxley clearly, as well as our surroundings.

In the clearing, I noticed that when I looked up, I could see the bright bulbs twinkling against the night sky. Without the light pollution, the stars were easily seen and illuminated the blue-black sky in scattered brilliance.

"Wow," I whispered in awe. It was absolutely beautiful.

Jacob migrated over to a trunk that sat at the base of a tree then unfolded a blanket from it and placed it on the ground. He then grabbed my hand and guided me onto the blanket.

"The green is the toxic carbon dioxide released from the trees in the Deadlands. It's very dangerous, but from down here it looks beautiful," Kemper explained while pointing up at the sky. I watched as the green haze danced in the dark.

"When we were boys, before we all lived together, we'd sneak away from home and meet here," Kemper explained while I got comfortable. Once I was situated, Jacob laid down on my right, and Kemper on my left. Huxley sat cross-legged at my feet, but I felt the warm touch of his hand rest against my ankle. The feather-light brush of his skin against mine was so soft, I wouldn't have noticed him if it weren't for the intense electricity that bounced between us.

"Our parents all knew where we were. We weren't nearly as good at sneaking around as we are now," Jacob said with a chuckle.

"How'd you find it?" I asked. I wondered if the grove was as beautiful during the day as it was at night.

"Wanna tell that story, Hux?" Kemper asked. He looped his pinkie through mine and squeezed. I loved the little touches he gave me and squeezed him back.

"Patrick and I didn't always get along, especially when we were really young. We were always fighting over something stupid, and our mother was always tanning our asses, with our Father's belt, over it. One night, we got into a big fight. I don't even know what it was about, but I remember Patrick crying and running away," Huxley explained, scooting closer to me.

"Normally, when he runs off, he'd show back up in a couple of hours, and we'd be back to annoying the hell out of each other." Huxley's coarse fingers began lightly tracing designs upon my leg, causing me to shiver despite the warm weather. "But this time, he didn't show back up." Jacob then gripped my hand and the feeling of touching all three of them, sent my heart into overdrive.

"I didn't want our parents to know we were fighting, so I got the others, and we went looking for him," Huxley said with a sigh.

"Cyler was learning how to track, so after hours of worrying and following his lead, we ended up finding him here," Kemper added. I tried to imagine what each of them looked like as young boys and smiled. It made sense that Cyler would take charge. Even then, he was their leader.

"We weren't expecting to find Patrick in the middle of a standoff with a big motherfucking bear!" Jacob said loudly, causing me to jump. Were there bears out here? Oh no, no, no! I started to sit up, determined to get out of that dark and terrifying grove as quickly as possible .

"Oh, calm down. There hasn't been a bear spotted in these woods for years, not since that night. They mostly stick to the Deadlands," Huxley assured me in what I think he intended to be a calm tone.

"Cyler, being the idiot that he is, started to run at the bear while screaming and clapping his hands," Huxley said. The image made me snort loudly, causing the guys to chuckle, too.

"And because we all blindly followed everything Cyler did, we all started charging the bear while screaming, too," Kemper added.

"The bear ran off, probably confused as hell as to what just happened, but we felt like gods," Jacob said with a smile.

"We're better together, that's for sure," Kemper said, with a seriousness to his tone that reverberated around us. I wanted to dissect his statement and apply it to my current situation with them all but disallowed my mind to tread those waters.

"Aside from us, you're the only one that we've ever brought here," Huxley whispered, as though he was scared at the implications of my presence here. His fingers stopped lazily tracing along my ankle, and I missed the comfort he provided, even though it still confused me. His whiplash of affections reminded me of a time that I allowed myself to be used, and I was determined to figure out what side of the line between hate and like I was on with him.

"Well, I won't tell anyone. It can be our little secret," I began. "But I guess this means, you're gonna have to admit that you don't hate me anymore, Hux," I said in what I hoped came across as a joke.

Jacob and Kemper stilled beside me, and I wondered if what I said was wrong. If I overstepped a boundary or triggered an insecurity within Huxley somehow.

"We both know I haven't hated you for a while now, Ash." That was all Huxley said. I felt Jacob and Kemper relax suddenly. It seemed that they, too, felt invested in Huxley's feelings towards me. His opinion mattered, and they wanted this to work. Whatever *this* was.

CHAPTER NINETEEN

T he next two days I kept busy working at the General Store and cleaning Black Manor. Any idle moment was spent consumed with worry for Cyler and Patrick or obsessing over my more-than-friendly relationship with the guys.

On the third day, I woke up in Huxley's bed. He had guard shift last night, and it was the first time I felt comfortable enough in my friendship with him to invade his personal space. His brown bedding smelled like evergreen and spice, and I caught myself breathing in the scent multiple times throughout the night.

I enjoyed a lazy morning. The Bakery was closed during the weekend, so I spent my time keeping busy and not worrying about Cyler and Patrick by making donuts and carrot cake; two items I hoped to add to the Bakery's menu very soon.

After that, I went to my old room to paint. It was still recovering from Jules' tantrum. Even though most of my supplies were ruined by her, I still managed to find a canvas and some paint that wasn't completely destroyed. After clearing a spot and texting Cyler a reminder that we really needed to get the room cleaned so I could stop bed hopping, I started to paint the grove from last night .

The dark sky etched in my mind's eye and the importance of that special place burned into my memory. I wanted to bring a bit of the grove back to the Black Manor. I let the calm and familiarity of the place guide my brushstrokes. I painted the grass floor and the moonlight illuminating the space.

While painting, I heard a commotion erupt in the kitchen. I abandoned my project to investigate, praying that Jules wasn't back and causing havoc. In the kitchen, I saw Jacob pacing the floor, while Tallis sat at the head of our table with a pensive expression. Maverick had his arms crossed over his chest and was shaking his head.

"How the fuck did this even happen?!" Hux growled out.

"I'm not sure, their tablets are offline, and I lost

their GPS signal sometime late last night. I assumed they had poor signal, but now, I think something's happened," Maverick said with a choke.

"Wh-what's going on?" I stuttered.

"Cyler and Patrick are . . . missing," Kemper said in a soft tone while thrusting his fists into his slacks and rocking on his toes. He looked nervous and scared. I reflexively grabbed my chest as pain rocked through me. I collapsed under the worry and found the nearest seat to break down in. Patrick and Cyler were in danger.

"They went missing early this morning. I was periodically checking their signal, and when I noticed that they went completely off the grid, I ran a few more scans, but . . . they're gone," Maverick said with slumped shoulders. I looked around the room in disbelief.

"How could they just disappear? This isn't possible," I asked, praying that this was all just one big joke.

"People don't disappear, *Agrio.* " Tallis said in a morbid tone while picking at a scab on his stark white knuckle.

I realized with certainty that he was right. Most likely, Cyler and Patrick were abducted. I couldn't help but assume the worst. They were either hurt, or dead.

"We have to do something," I said while standing up on shaky legs. Maverick looked at me with profound sadness, and my heart broke .

"I'll go get Mia," Jacob said while lacing his shoes. "We need to come up with a plan."

"Maverick, you work on finding out where they are. Check every damn radio wave out there if you have to. Tallis, go with Jacob. Kemper, stay here. We need to prepare to leave by nightfall."

"Where are we going?" I asked with newfound determination.

"*You* aren't going anywhere. *We* are paying emperorLackley a little visit," Huxley said, and everyone stared at him for a moment, seemingly in shock by his newfound authority. "Come *on* . Let's *move* ," he ordered. Everyone scattered into different directions, and before I could orient myself, the kitchen was empty.

"Come on," Huxley ordered, while grabbing my hand and pulling me upstairs to his room.

"Where are we going?" I asked.

Huxley huffed while kicking open his door and moving me towards the wingback chair in the corner of his room. He found a black leather bag then started calmly loading it with various supplies.

Once he was satisfied that he had everything he needed, he sat on his bed. The plush comforter was a stark difference to his rigid posture and grim demeanor. I stood and began pacing the floor. With each step and tick of the clock I wondered if Cyler and Patrick were still alive. If they were being tortured. If Josiah was behind this.

"Will you stop doing that? I'm trying to think," Huxley growled while massaging his temples.

I ignored him.

"Shouldn't Jacob be back by now? I should check on him. Maybe he got stopped somewhere," I thought out loud while continuing to pace.

I felt an anxious energy that propelled me to keep moving. Keep talking. Anything to keep myself from thinking. Since the moment I heard of their disappearance, my mind had become a continuous loop of worry.

"Yes, yes. I—I think I'll go check on Jacob. He could have gotten lost. Or maybe he got hurt on his way to the Scavenger camp. That's it. I can't sit here. I'll go find him. That's what I'll— "

"Ash! Sit your pretty ass down and stop talking. I'm trying to come up with a plan that doesn't involve us dying, and your stupid rambling is going to drive me crazy." I watched as Huxley gripped his knees and stared at me with a look of utter frustration. His hair was wild and matched the lightning that danced across his green, piercing eyes.

"Well, I'm just so sorry that I can't be as emotionless as you!" I screamed, needing to release some of my worry, fears, and frustration onto someone.

Huxley stood and stalked his way over to me, and I flinched at his aggressive movements. Once in front of me, his familiar scent filled me. My nose was just inches from his defined chest, and if I wasn't so mad at him right now, I might have sought the comfort of his arms. I needed to be held. To be reassured. But I surely didn't need Huxley. I needed Cyler and Patrick to be home, safe and sound.

"I love them, Huxley. I can't lose them," I sobbed while my resolved crumbled, and all my fears began suffocating me. I felt my anxiety and inner turmoil begin to snake itself around my throat like icy vines.

Huxley gripped my shoulders and stared at me. His thick fingers were steadying and firm, as though he was trying to stop me from jumping off the emotional ledge I was on. I saw a flash of pain and uncertainty in his eyes before he shook them away.

Huxley then bent over slightly and pulled me to him before claiming my lips with his own.

His lips were cold and trembled with the emotion bouncing between us. Shock was my first reaction, but quickly that feeling faded and a totally new sensation took its place.

Lust. Want. Need.

Huxley kissed me with such certainty that I had no choice but to fall a bit for him in that moment. His lips moved against mine with a force that I felt *everywhere*. His hands slid down my bare arms, leaving waves of tingles beneath them until he grabbed my waist and pushed closer to me. Our hips rocked like waves against one another. Between kisses, I gasped and whispered out. "What are you doing?"

My back hit his bedroom wall, and in one swift moment, my hands were anchored to my side, preventing them from roaming the large muscles on his back like I ached to do.

A low moan grumbled within his chest. "Can't you tell? I'm fucking kissing you, Ash." He continued to move his lips against mine in frantic movements, as if he wanted to drink every last drop of this moment and savor it.

After what felt like hours, he sucked on my

bottom lip before exhaling a slow and steady breath. Huxley then slowly pushed me away in a strained display of control. I saw the protruding veins in his arms throb with the evidence of what we just did.

"Now. Sit here and be quiet like a good little Walker," he said, his voice hoarse. With a smirk, he walked back over to his bed and plopped down in a lying position. He threw a thick forearm over his eyes and sighed in contentment. He looked completely relaxed, and my heart was crushed at how unaffected he was.

I felt unsure of what just happened. Hux *kissed* me. I mean *really* kissed me. What did this mean? Why now? My shaky legs and pounding heart ached for rest. I traveled to the corner of the room where his recliner was and sat down, silently agonizing over what just happened between us.

"Ahhh, much better," Huxley said with a chuckle.

Realization washed over me. The kiss was a distraction. A cheap ploy to get me to stop talking. If Huxley wanted me to calm down that *definitely* wasn't the way to do it. I muttered, "Jackass," before walking out of his room and towards the living room.

I resumed pacing, but with much more vigor. I piled my anxiety about my and Huxley's kiss on top of the other worries that plagued me and stomped my feet loudly. Huxley couldn't have picked a worse time to mess with my head.

I spied my tablet on one of the recliners, and in a moment of weakness and determination, picked it up and called Josiah. I knew the guys would be furious at my actions, but I couldn't care less. I wanted answers. I wanted to feel like I was doing something that would aid in bringing back Cyler and Patrick.

Josiah answered it almost immediately, and I was greeted with a pained expression. It seemed to be what he wore daily now.

"Where are they, Josiah? I know you know." I was foregoing pleasantries and jumping right into the situation at hand.

"Ash—" Josiah began, but I saw his bullshit excuse a mile away and cut him off.

"Don't even start with me right now, Josiah!" I roared in a tone that momentarily shocked us both. "You know where Cyler and Patrick are. You know what emperorLackley is planning. Tell me. Right. Now."

Josiah's shocked eyes, which were the size of disks, fueled my anger. It felt ridiculously good to let loose the repressed frustrations I've been feeling.

"I can't help you, Ashleigh. He'll punish me,"

Josiah said in a defeated voice.

"So help me, Josiah—"

"Who are you–?"

He cut me off and his face grew red with frustration. "The Ash I know would trust that I'm doing what I can! It's not that easy!"

"The Ash you know is gone, Josiah," I replied almost instantly. "I'm done worshiping every move you make. Tell me where they are. *Please.* If you ever loved me—ever felt a sliver of what I felt for you— you'll help me," I pleaded as tears streamed down my face.

"I can't, Ashleigh."

The silence between us stretched into a large black hole that ate up whatever lingering love I felt for Josiah. I straightened my spine and peered at him with a newfound resolve that charged my hatred for him.

"Josiah, I want you to look at me," I said in an eerily calm voice. His eyes flashed to mine. "I want you to remember everything about this moment. Catalogue it in the deepest parts of your heart, in the deepest recesses of your memories of me, each and every little detail. Because years from now, when you wonder what happened to the girl that you once knew, the girl that *worshiped* you. The girl that was your best friend. The girl that *loved* you. You'll be able to vividly remember that it was right here, right now, when you completely lost her."

I clicked the tablet off and threw it across the room. It shattered against the wall, and I crumbled to the floor in a heap of sadness and relief. It was over. It was *really* over.

A hot hand rested on my shoulder as I sobbed, and I turned my head to see who was trying to comfort me. Jacob.

"Ash, sweetie. Tallis and Mia are downstairs," he said in a tentative voice. I looked around and saw Huxley looking at me with profound—guilt? And Kemper looked almost happy. They must have seen and heard everything.

"He wouldn't help me," I murmured. "He wouldn't tell me where they are."

Jacob's fingers drifted to my face and he placed a warm, lingering kiss on my forehead before looking deep into my eyes. "We'll find them, Ash. I promise. Let's go get them back."

I wrapped my arm around his, and together we made our way downstairs, followed by Kemper and Huxley. My heart thudded both clumsily and joyfully at the sudden freedom that Josiah's betrayal left behind.

CHAPTER TWENTY

Josiah 18 Months Ago

J osiah!" a loud voice echoed throughout Stonewell Manor.

I was working at my desk when Father came bounding through my bedroom door with a ridiculous grin on his face. His cheeks were flushed, his breath reeked of whiskey. I set my tablet down as his pudgy body swayed from side to side, the ripples of his movements jiggling his flesh.

"I've got good news, my boy," he said with an exhale while plopping onto my bed and shuffling off his boots. "I figured it out—right oh, I did! I figured out a sooooo-loution," he slurred.

I faced him with a bored expression, I was quite

used to his drunk excursions and rambling. "And what sooooo-loution have you figured out?" I asked, my tone mocking. I adjusted my glasses and sent a message to Ash. When he was drunk like this, it was best that she kept hidden.

"Our debts, Josiah! Our debts will be forgiven. Once I send this pesky message to the Emperor!" he exclaimed while using his greasy index finger to type out a message. I considered allowing him to embarrass himself with a drunk message to emperorLackley, but still swiped it from his clumsy fingers before he could hit send. I peered down at the tablet and saw one letter—X.

"What does Influenza X have to do with this?" I asked immediately, wishing I could snap my fingers and Father would sober up.

Father let loose a big belly laugh and his shoulders shook with the force of it.

"Everything has to do with it, Boy. *Everything.*"

I stood and waltzed over to him and forced myself to endure his breath and address him at eye level. "Explain."

"I know what Lackley's done. I know what he's planning to do." Father shrugged, leaning back onto my bed. I noticed that he was so drunk that his pants were soiled. I cringed. Ashleigh would have to wash my sheets tonight.

"What are you saying?" I persisted. I needed to know exactly what he knew and if he had already told anyone. My father loved to spout conspiracy theories, and his credibility had steadily declined in the previous years.

Father's eyelids fluttered shut, and I poked him with a sturdy finger, jolting him awake. He flailed his arms and hit me. It wasn't the worst his fists have ever done, but it would leave a bruise.

"What do you want, boy?" he sneered. Drops of saliva puffed out of his cracked lips.

"What are you planning?" I balled my hands into a fist and tried not to scream.

"Lackley is in deep shit!" Father finally got his pants unbuttoned, but he decided that pushing his pants down was too much effort, so he gave up. I was desperate to keep him awake so I could hear what he had to say, therefore I helped him shimmy his encompassing frame out of his black, soiled slacks.

"The greedy fool! We're all ticking time bombs!" he roared while jolting up into a sitting position and pulling me close. His fist clutched my button-down shirt, and I cringed, all too familiar with his drunken force.

"The Governor's right-hand man told me himself. We'll all be vaccine rejects soon—that's right! Haven't you wondered why more and more people are rejecting the Vaccinations?" Father was whispering now. As if worried someone was listening in on our conversation. "Lackley would pay a pretty penny to keep news like this from getting out!" Father now chuckled with such malice that my eyes widened. I couldn't let this happen. Lackley wouldn't pay my father a dime. He'd simply kill us.

I knew this day was coming. We had been preparing for quite some time now. I was warned that Father was getting too close. He was too curious. Too *greedy*.

"I know Lackley's deepest secret," Father said with a slightly giddy yawn.

I watched him slump back onto my bed and close his eyes.

"Get some rest, Father," I said in a calm voice.

I knew what had to be done. What should have been done years ago, when his fist first became acquainted with my flesh. When he first started noticing Ashleigh's body. When Mother first started crying at night. My Father was a stain on society. A waste of oxygen.

Going to war with emperorLackley would surely

result in my family's death. In Ashleigh's death. It's why I made preparations long ago.

Father's been a loose cannon for too long.

It ended now.

Within moments he was passed out and snoring quietly against the pillow. I took a moment to watch my drunken mess of a father sleep peacefully. While asleep, he wasn't a threat. He wasn't gambling or shoving Mother down the stairs or leering at Ashleigh. He looked almost like what a Father was supposed to be.

But I knew better.

I grabbed the pillow next to him and after a moment's pause, placed it over his face and pressed down *hard* . At first he didn't move. His deep and drunk slumber caused him to feel no pain. I don't think he felt the fire in his lungs as they burned for air. Or the last few pounding beats of his heart, before the blood simply stopped flowing. He twitched a few times, the last bit of electricity zapping his now dead neurons as he kissed eternity and finally left us.

I enjoyed watching the last little sparks of life flee his worthless body.

I left the door open, so he'd be easy to find. Mother would be home soon from her afternoon tea at the Carmichaels'. I didn't want the carnage in my room for longer than necessary.

I washed my hands in the kitchen sink, and before slipping outside, I sent a message to my contact. Within three minutes, emperorLackley was ringing my tablet.

"It's done," I answered. "Your right-hand man told him. No one else knows."

"Right oh, my boy. I'm glad we could mutually benefit from this," he cooed before ending the call with a click.

The warmth of the sun spurred me further, and I walked with a bit of a bounce to my step towards the park.

The weather was divine, and I enjoyed the crisp air. It was a beautiful day for a walk.

CHAPTER TWENTY-ONE

Ashleigh Present Day

I packed a small bag with stoic determination, while preparing my speech to Huxley as to why I should travel with them. No kiss could distract me from being there for Cyler and Patrick. Especially kisses meant as a distraction tactic—that *jerk*.

Maverick discovered whispers of hope that Cyler and Patrick were in Galla, which was a fairly anticlimactic discovery. A storefront security camera down the street from the Stonewell Manor caught a glimpse of a government transport zooming by with tinted windows, and a quick heat signature showed two figures handcuffed in the back. I wanted to punch something. Josiah was behind this, I just *knew* it.

They all sat around the kitchen, each of them looking at tablets, trying to come up with a plan. Tallis observed them with a smirk while he picked his nails.

"We should just ambush them!" Jacob suggested with fierce eyes that slid across the room with intent. He twitched and seemed eager to act.

"Oh yes, then we can be abducted or killed, too. Brilliant plan, Jacob. Well done," Huxley said with an eye-roll .

"They'll be heavily guarded. There's no way we can out man them. We need reinforcements," Kemper said matter-of-factly. He peered at Tallis, as if hoping he could offer support.

"The other tribes are still deliberating on even meeting with Cyler, let alone manning a rescue mission for him. I can only offer what men I have, and that still wouldn't be enough," Tallis replied. I noticed how he carried himself with calm certainty. He didn't seem bothered by this at all. He acted as though he was merely intrigued by the problem.

Huxley continued to rewind and replay the footage at the shop while Maverick and Kemp whispered in the corner. Mia sharpened her blade with precision and kept silent and pensive. She was on high alert and observed the room with a stoic glare.

The front door slammed, and I looked up to see a very flustered but still beautiful Jules strolling into the kitchen. The entire room groaned in frustration.

"Oh my! Don't act so excited to see me!" she exclaimed while plopping down on a vacant chair next to Mia. The two of them exchanged mutual scowls before Jules rolled her eyes and scraped her chair across the hard wood floor farther away from her.

"So what are you doing to get my brother back?" she asked without a trace of malice. She *almost* sounded genuinely concerned about his wellbeing, which surprised me.

Once again, I looked around the room, praying that someone would come up with a plan to rescue Cyler and Patrick. Something that didn't involve us getting hurt, too.

Jules huffed. "Oh, the silence is super reassuring. This is a great plan. Just sit here quietly until they just magically appear," she said while picking the paint off her nails. The gesture was a nervous tick I noticed she had in our few encounters.

"How did you even know they were gone?" Jacob asked with a sigh, leaning forward on his elbows.

They both exchanged a sad look that seemed different from the other times I observed their interactions. Something had changed between them, and I wasn't sure how it made me feel.

"Well, it's no thanks to you lot! It's a small Providence, word travels fast. I had to find out from Tallis that my own brother was abducted. I can't believe you didn't think to tell me Mav, after everything our family has been through!" Her screeching elevated the tension in the room to critical levels.

Everyone stared at Tallis who shrugged under their scrutiny. He lifted the right side of his lips in a brief but mischievous smile towards Jules.

"I just can't believe you didn't tell me. You never tell me anything, Mav. I've always been on the outs," she complained with her chin raised as she looked down her nose at everyone.

I wanted to feel sorry for Jules in that moment but found it hard. Once again, she was finding a way to make herself the center of attention, when in reality we needed support, not another fight. I expected the tense Maverick to snap at Jules, but instead he collapsed at the table and grasped her hands.

"I'm sorry, Jules. I know we're a fucked up family, but we'll get him back. We just need to figure out how to get into the Stonewell Manor undetect-ed," he said, surprisingly calm.

"Well that's easy!" she exclaimed in an overly chipper voice. She then glanced around the room before staring at me with such self-righteous glee that I had to swallow the rage that bubbled up inside of me.

"You," she began while flipping her black hair over her bony shoulder and sighing. She enjoyed having everyone hanging on to her every word. "... need a distraction. I've been reading the tabloids. There has been a lot of civil unrest in the Walker Zones these days. It would be such a shame if one of their little protests got out of hand." She shrugged and continued to pick at her nails, feigning indiffer-ence, but I saw the burning determination under-neath. Despite everything that had happened between her and the guys, she still *cared* for them in ways that I didn't quite understand .

"We could spur a riot in the Zone," I began hurriedly, while clinging to the coattails of what Jules suggested and running with it. "Once the Arches are preoccupied with that, we can make our way to the Stonewell Manor."

"I mean, that's basically what I already suggested

but sure, go ahead and run with *my* plan," Jules scoffed.

I noticed Mia hold a hand over her mouth to stifle a chuckle.

"We don't even know that they're at the Stonewell Manor," Maverick added while rubbing his eyes. I saw the worry lines on his brows and my heart seized.

"I can almost guarantee that even if they aren't there, Josiah knows where they are," I said while bunching the edges of my skirt into my fist before pinching my thigh.

"Are you prepared to face him?" Kemper asked softly, walking over to me. He placed his hand upon my shoulder before kneeling down and peering at me with his intense blue eyes that kissed the edges of my soul.

"I'll do anything to get Cyler and Patrick back," I whispered. I tried to fight back the tears that gathered in the pockets of my eyelids.

"Well great, now that that's settled, when are we going?" Mia, who until now had been quiet, asked. She sheathed her knife after pointing it threateningly at Jules who had just opened her mouth to speak before promptly closing it at Mia's unspoken threat.

Tallis gave Mia a disapproving look while taking a drink of his water.

"*We* aren't going anywhere. Jules and Ash are staying here while we get this plan mobilized," Huxley growled.

I gave him a pointed stare.

"Well I guess you can figure out how to navigate Galla as well as find Josiah on your own then," I began. "You must know everywhere he frequents. Do you plan on chopping off my thumb to use my fingerprint for his door scanner?"

Huxley retreated into his usual emotional hibernation as I pointed out each reason as to why I should go with them. It was unlikely that Josiah had changed the locks on their door, which meant that I was the only person in this room that could easily get in.

"I don't know, Ashleigh," Maverick muttered while scratching his neck. "I think Huxley might be right. You aren't necessarily trained for something like this, and we'd all be worrying about keeping you safe instead of being focused on the mission."

"Oh shut up already, you fussy hens. Ash is a big girl, and I'll keep her safe. You both know she's an asset on this mission. No one else knows the ins and outs of

Josiah's whereabouts like her," Mia said while standing. "I'm tired of waiting. We're wasting time, and
Galla is at *least* a two-day ride from here at max speeds
on a transport." Mia grabbed the crook of my arm and
grabbed the back pack I had prepared and hidden
under the table, swinging it over her shoulder. "Let's
go, boys!" She pulled me towards the kitchen's exit.

I turned to see if they were following, just in time
to see Jules clutching Maverick and Jacob in a group
hug. She was whispering in Jacob's ear, and I wanted
to yank her snake-like fingers off of him, but I knew
that now wasn't the right time for jealousy. Regardless of the pain bound to their relationship, there was
still history between all of them and Jules. We had a
mission to fine tune, but still, the foolish agony I saw
when they were together made my heart squeeze
with tension.

We crammed into the small transport after
careful maneuvering and losing one of Mia's three
bags of weapons. Maverick typed in our coordinates
on the transport's dash, and we jolted forward
with ease.

"We'll have to pass through the capital to get to
Galla," he said with a sigh. I was worried about traveling through emperorLackley's domain.

"Can we go around?" I asked, already fearing the answer.

"Not without adding another day to our trip," Kemper answered. "The Capital is the halfway point between here and Galla. We'll just have to be sure and slip through unnoticed."

"Don't they have checkpoints?" I asked, wondering how we would get through without emperorLackley noticing .

"I know a way through the Capital that'll keep us off their radar," Tallis said. He put his arms behind his head and stretched out in the cramped space for a nap. I noticed the eerily calm way he approached all of this with scrutiny.

What kind of person could be so nonchalant about all of this?

"Just wake me up when we're about an hour outside of the gates," he added with a yawn, ending the conversation.

I grabbed Maverick's rough hand and gripped it anxiously. I knew that we still had unresolved tension to settle between us thanks to Cyler's democratic trade deal decision with Ethros, but I craved his contact and reassurance. As Maverick settled into his leather bucket seat, Huxley's eyes focused on my and

Maverick's enclosed hands, and I cringed at the hostility reflected in his stare.

Huxley crossed his arms across his broad chest and scowled as he bit the corner of his lip in frustration. "Can we get this fucking transport to move faster please?"

Mia observed us all with a grin and rolled her eyes before inconspicuously holding up six fingers with a wink. I blushed.

"How are we going to cause a riot in the Walker Zone?" I asked. I felt the compulsive desire to define every aspect of this mission and prepare. I felt out of control and the uncertainty of it all made me want to scream.

"I packed a lovely little makeshift bomb. It's a *bit* temperamental, but will do the job," Mia said with a shrug. For a brief moment, we all paused in shocked disbelief, but soon everyone immediately began talking at once.

"You brought a BOMB aboard the transport?" Maverick gasped while releasing my hand. He started rummaging through bags on the floorboard until he found one with dynamite and wires. He snapped back into his seat with his hands in the air once he found it.

"A temperamental bomb?" Jacob added with

equal shock.

"Will you all please keep it down, I'm trying to rest. It's just a little bomb, nothing to lose sleep over," Tallis said while readjusting his arms to get more comfortable. "In fact, it was Jules that suggested it. She fetched it from my tent for me," he added in a wistful tone that hinted he admired Jules for more than just her ability to come up with a good plan. I wondered how well they knew one another. They were such opposites.

Maverick gave me a small half-smile then began flipping through his tablet, watching and re-watching the security footage and trying to make sense of it all. I wanted to comfort him. I wanted to resolve the pain and hurt between us, but I bit my tongue and let him work, while silently agonizing over what the next few days would bring.

The transport remained in eloquent silence aside from the occasional question and the Chief's light snores. Hours passed, and the surmounting anxiety within me caused my flinching fingers to continuously pinch my thigh.

Occasionally, I looked outside at the abandoned buildings and wasted cities. I catalogued the images in my mind's eye as we passed all the emptiness of the Empire that echoed how my heart currently felt.

Cyler and Patrick's lingering absence was like an uncomfortable itch. I couldn't relax my mind long enough to sleep, and I felt rigid next to Maverick. I still felt unsure of where we stood since our differing views on Heat, especially now that it led to Cyler and Patrick's abduction. I wanted to lean against his shoulder and slip into a comforting sleep but remained firm and rod-straight in my leather seat, avoiding all contact despite the warmth that came off of him in waves of temptation.

"Come here, sweetheart," Jacob cooed while shoving Kemper and indicating that we should switch spots. With careful maneuvering, I crossed the transport and sank into the seat beside him. He wormed my legs over his lap and cradled me. "You need to rest, Ash," he whispered into my ear in a low tone intended only for me.

"I—I can't," I replied with a cracked voice. His large hands migrated to my boots and he slowly worked their brown laces before slipping them off. They fell to the floor of the transport with a thud, but no one paid us much mind. His fingers roamed over my legs and feet in circular motions with a medium pressure. *"Relax,"* he breathed out. "We'll find them."

"What if we don't?" I asked. The question made

pain radiate throughout my chest. "If something happened to them, Jacob, I don't know what I'd do."

Jacob's warm scent and calming movements continued as he remained in pensive silence. "Ash," he began, and I stiffened at the tone of it. His voice seemed detached. "I know Cyler and Patrick better than anyone. They'll do everything in their power to come back to you—to us," he choked out.

"I never–" I began before biting my tongue.

"You never what?" Jacob probed. His fingers stopped their comforting massage, and I blinked back tears.

"I never got to tell them . . ." I drifted off in embarrassment. I noticed that Huxley was listening to me now, and I couldn't—no— wouldn't finish the regretful thoughts that were poisoning my mind.

I never got to tell them how I felt. How they made me feel. How Cyler's touches felt like pure, unadulterated freedom and comfort. Or how Patrick's smile made my heart race with giddy antici-pation, and I could spend eternity in his arms.

"Sweetheart," Jacob replied. "They know. We *all* know."

The slow massage made me feel drowsy with desire, and slowly, ever so slowly, I fell into a deep sleep.

CHAPTER TWENTY-TWO

A shleigh, wake up," a soft voice murmured. My eyes opened, and I rolled my neck to work out the uncomfortable kinks that plagued my joints. "We're an hour outside of the Capital, and we need to refuel. Tallis is taking us in through an abandoned entrance, but we need to remain diligent," Kemper explained with kind but tired eyes.

I observed him in a daze while sitting up. His shirt was wrinkled from sitting in the transport. My eyes shifted to find Jacob awake and eyeing me with appreciation. My hair felt wild from sleep, and my shirt was loose and stretched out, revealing my healthy cleavage.

I looked outside and was greeted by vast, sandy emptiness. Dust kicked up from beneath the transport, and I noticed a looming metropolis in the distance. Tall towers and bright lights illuminated the night sky, like a beacon in the wasteland.

"You and Mia need to change into clothes more suited for the Capital," Huxley said. "You'll stick out like a sore thumb wearing *that* ." Hux nodded at me, and I adjusted my shirt to cover up my chest. The movement caused Kemper to blush.

"I grabbed some extra clothes before leaving," Kemper said with a cautious smile before rummaging through his pack and throwing two dresses at me. The thick velvet material that I once adored and longed for, now felt heavy and limiting.

Mia scrunched her nose and peered at the dresses like they were going to burst into flames at any moment. "I'll never understand Capital fashion. How the fuck am I supposed to stab someone while wearing this?" she asked while clicking her tongue and pulling at the seams, as if trying to stretch it out more.

"You'll need to go ahead and get changed. We will be there within the hour," Kemper choked out awkwardly while giving me an appreciative look. The thought of changing clothes in this cramped transport made me blush in embarrassment.

However, the ever confident Mia simply slipped

off her tight shirt and casually shimmied out of her charcoal leather pants. Everyone averted their eyes in polite discomfort.

"I didn't think Dormas men were such *prudes,*" she joked with a snort while buttoning the collar of the maroon dress. She looked completely unlike herself in that moment. She almost looked like an elite.

I looked around the transport as everyone shifted and coughed in discomfort. There wasn't much time for me to feel ashamed of changing clothes in front of them, so I simply followed Mia's lead. Except my efforts lacked the swiftness of Mia's movements, and I had *much* less enthusiasm. In many ways, I had evolved past my prude Galla habits, but I still had moments of unyielding modesty.

My shirt got caught in my hair, and my skirt twisted around my legs as I tried to work it off of my round hips. Soon, I felt out of breath and had to pause my untangling to catch it.

"Keep your fucking eyes to the ceiling, Tallis," Huxley said in a low, threatening tone. My chest rose and fell as I paused and looked up from my twisted skirt to see four pairs of eyes glued to me.

"Believe me, I'm watching out of pure amusement. She's a clumsy one. Can I request her for someone else's ambush team?" Tallis asked jokingly .

"Oh shut up," Huxley said while rolling his eyes, but I saw how the right corner of his lip lifted in amusement.

"If you're going to stare, one of you might as well help the poor girl. My *Agrio* is a mess," Mia said with a snort while strapping a knife to her toned thigh. "Think I could cut a slit in this?" she asked to no one in particular.

The transport was shaped like a rectangle, with leather benches on each side, leaving the middle open. Kemper made his way towards me and kneeled at my feet. He slowly worked the skirt off of me in teasingly slow strides. Once it was no longer tangled around me, Jacob helped me into the thick and encompassing dress, styled in the normal Empirical fashion.

"Can one of you tie the bodice?" I asked in a whisper. The transport felt hot. Maverick looked up at me, and I briefly wondered if he would allow this grudge to continue, or if he would help me. After a pause, he set aside his tablet and motioned me near. With the practiced movements of a surgeon, he slowly tightened the laced strings upon my back. I felt his feather-light fingertips along my spine, and I shivered under his attentive contact. He softly squeezed my hips to indicate he was done, and I shuffled on my knees back to my seat by Jacob as I tried to slow my breath.

I wasn't sure if it was the too-tight dress, the intense stares of the boys, or my increasing anxiety, but it felt like a heavy weight was on my chest. "How are we sneaking through the Capital again?" I asked in a breathy tone.

"Scavengers have created an underground trade route to get Walkers to the Deadlands, we also use it to gather supplies. One of my contacts is there. We can go and refuel, then get on our way," Tallis explained while braiding his long white hair and pulling it into a rimmed hat.

"How long have you been using this underground trade route?" I asked. Everything I've witnessed thus far has showed me that Scavengers were ridiculously resourceful.

"Since we've been in the Deadlands, *Agrio,* " Mia answered. " Being banished has its perks, but we had to get a little *creative,* so to speak."

"We do what we have to. We survive," Tallis said while looking at me with his fierce eyes. His lips were cracked, and I saw the flash of his sharp teeth as he bit them.

"Do you think your people made the right decision to escape the Zone and move to the Deadlands?" I asked bravely. The options available to those that couldn't afford the vaccine were limited. Be bought by an elite family, move to the Zone, or escape to the Deadlands. None of those seemed sustainable or worthwhile. The world was cruel.

"I don't think there is a right decision anymore," Mia said with a frown. She too seemed to contemplate the unfairness of it all.

"I think Dormas is the right place. If I could move everyone safely there, I would," I said.

As we approached the city, I noticed the impressive towers covered in digital screens and felt significantly out of place. I had grown to love the simplicity of Dormas, and the overbearing buildings that stood over the city felt like mountains of machinery. Once close enough, Tallis took control of the transport's dash and directed us towards the east, a much less established area of the city.

"Hope you don't mind, we will be traveling a *bit* off the usual path. Emperor Lackley has patrol units on every road leading into the city but lacks surveillance on the eastern side. He's either arrogant or is lacking manpower these days," Tallis said while pushing us off the road and towards a tall, wired fence in a darkly lit area.

"So, where is this mystical entrance you bragged about?" Huxley mused with a scowl. He didn't seem impressed by the Scavenger chief in the slightest.

"Keep watching," Tallis replied.

We continued to plow forward towards the fence at fast speeds, and I felt the tight grip of fear lodge itself in my throat. We were going to hit the fence. We were going to *crash*.

"Alright, Tallis, the game is up, time to slow down now," Jacob joked while leaning on the edge of his seat. He appeared ready to take over the dashboard at a moment's notice. Tallis merely ignored him.

"Hey, we need to slow down, we're gonna hit the fence!" Maverick yelled, he too seemed ready to get up and tackle him to regain control of the transport.

"Calm down, he's got this under control," Mia said while buckling her seatbelt. We continued to surge forward, and before anyone else could complain, we blazed through the fence, as if it was made of mist. The entire transport exhaled in relief, with the exception of Mia and Tallis.

"It's a hologram," Kemper said in awe. A small

section of the fence, large enough to fit a transport, wavered, then came back into focus.

"My friend designed it. Brilliant, huh?" Tallis asked with a chuckle.

"You could have fucking warned us," Huxley groaned while looking at me. "You okay?" he asked.

"I've been better," I replied while running my hands along my thighs, reassuring myself that we didn't just crash, that I was still miraculously alive.

We drove through The Confederation of Dasos' capital center, and I peered at the people walking along the street. Men in top hats and suits got their morning coffee from automated dispensaries that flickered bright advertisements while they waited for their cup to brew.

I noticed a few Walkers wearing bright ear tags darting between traffic, carrying various armloads of groceries. The Confederation of Dasos was just like Galla in their Walker practices, except they exported their remaining Walkers to Zones in neighboring Providences. Emperor Lackley didn't want any non-procured Walkers in his Capital.

"Where are we going?" I asked while shifting in my seat. I was eager for a brief relief from the crowded transport and needed to use the facilities. My stomach rumbled after my question, and I remembered that it had been a while since I had eaten.

"Not far from here. Our contact lives close to the government building," Tallis explained.

"Doesn't that seem a bit risky?" Kemper asked.

"Lackley is over-confident in his authority," Maverick answered. "He's so convinced in his system that he wouldn't think to find treason right under his nose, it's brilliant, actually." He shook his head, peering outside in disgust.

The transport pulled to a stop in front of a metal town house with long rectangular windows and a maroon door. It was three stories with a flat roof, typical for dignitaries and well-off families. In fact, it was almost identical to the Stonewell Manor, which made my heart clench. Familiar submissive feelings of unworthiness washed over me. I shivered in response.

We looked out of place, despite our wardrobe change. Prim men peered at us curiously while walking to work. The hot and thick dress that was tight against my frame was useless.

Huxley grabbed my hand, and I looked down at it in shock. "Keep close," he whispered. "Cy will kill me if I let anything happen to you."

"It's okay to admit you want to take care of me," I

replied slowly in a low whisper just as Tallis knocked on the door. Huxley tensed and gripped my hand tighter.

An older man wearing a bronze ear tag opened the door and bowed respectfully to Tallis. He had salt and pepper hair, a young smile, and bright grey eyes.

"Welcome. I'm Claude, the Walker of this home. Master Lux has been expecting you." He smiled and extended his arm, welcoming us inside.

I followed through the threshold as we were guided towards the sitting room. The room was completely covered in tones of navy and baby blue with gold accents. Plush couches and mahogany furniture filled the room .

I excused myself to freshen up in the bathroom, then traveled back towards the sitting room and found everyone casually lounging. Claude was resting on a chaise lounge with his feet propped up on the coffee table.

"Lux thinks more with his dick than with his brain," the man said with a chuckle. He wiped tears of laughter from his cheeks while Tallis poured him a small glass of amber liquid. "I've been smuggling goods and Walkers through this house for years while he's off gallivanting around the Empire!" he roared in a proud tone before shifting his eyes to me. "Oh, right dearie, I *do* most sincerely apologize for my language." He whipped out a handkerchief and dabbed his sweaty forehead. He wore a dark suit but his shirt was wrinkled and unbuttoned, as if he only partially cared about his station here.

"I'm not bothered by it, I live with this lot," I said while throwing a thumb in Huxley's direction, which made him scowl.

"What the fuck is that supposed to mean?" Huxley asked while crossing his arms over his chest.

"How'd you become a smuggler for Scavengers?" I asked, ignoring Huxley and taking a seat on the chase lounge next to Mia. She was also enjoying a tall glass of something that was clear and smelled like rubbing alcohol. She rested her head on my shoulder in contentment. Her eyes were hooded, and I wanted to chastise her for drinking before our mission but decided against it. Mia seemed to be the type to do whatever she wanted, and I didn't want to anger her *or* become a victim of her knife throwing skills.

Huxley paced the room while occasionally stretching his muscles and peering anxiously out the windows. Jacob stuffed his face with what appeared to be cookies, while Kemper and Maverick argued about something on their tablets.

"I've been a Procured Walker my entire life. I was born into it. In fact, my Holder is actually my half-brother," Claude said with a knowing smile. The implications of his statement made me gape at him. His Senior Master was his *father*.

"My mother caught our father's eye, but she was just a Walker. When I was born, she was banished to the Walker Zones in Galla, but I was allowed to stay —as a procured Walker, of course. I was the bastard son of a Congressional seat holder, so the most I could hope for was a life of servitude in exchange for the vaccine."

My heart sank, and I applied his life to mine and what *could* have happened if Josiah and I had explored a relationship together. Claude was proof that Walkers and the Elite didn't mix—there were too many variables. Too many casualties.

"When my Master died, Lux stopped pretending he cared about the family legacy and started traveling to all the Providences with lenient gambling and prostitution rules. I was bored in this big old house and decided to make friends with a few people that could let me live out my rebellious tendencies."

Claude gave me a grin before downing his drink. "You'll want to wait until after dark before traveling again. I've cloaked your transport's airwave signature, but I think you'll find less resistance at night; besides, you look like you could use some rest and a nice hot cup of tea, Mistress." The term made me flinch. I was *no* Mistress.

"Please call me Ash, Claude," I said politely. "And we can't stay here all day. Every second that passes something could be happening to Cyler and Patrick. We need to leave within the hour," I said while standing, to further my point. Mia slumped over on the couch and stretched out her legs comfortably.

"Love, Claude is right. It'll be easier to sneak out of here at night, and we'll be in Galla by tomorrow afternoon," Kemper said hesitantly while looking around the room for support. Jacob got up and grabbed my elbow.

"Ash," Jacob began. "Cyler and Patrick are going to be okay. We'll be useless if we're stopped traveling out of the city. Plus, we still need to refuel."

"Oh! Right-oh you are, Master Jacob, is it Jacob? Yes—well, I'll take your transport to the refueling station a few miles away and bring it back," Claude said with a wide smile. I noticed that food was stuck in the prominent gap in his teeth. Claude stood up and wobbled a bit, probably from the alcohol, and I was thankful that he needn't operate the transport since it simply drove itself.

Tallis noticed Claude's inability to walk a straight line and offered to go with him. After a few stumbles they both left the Manor.

"So, what now?" I asked while plopping back down on the chair. Mia's mouth was open, her soft snores filled the room.

"Now, we rest," Jacob replied with a yawn. He slumped down the side of the wall and jetted his muscular legs in front of him. Soon, he, too, was asleep. At first, I thought it was because he cradled me for the entirety of the trip here, but I noticed that the others were drooping with drowsiness.

"Are you all okay?" I asked while watching Maverick's head bob in his chair. "Hello?" I asked.

Before anyone could answer, the front door opened with a jolt, startling me. I stood to address whatever was attacking us, but just as I started to make out the tall frame of an armored man, I was shot with a piercing needle in my right leg. While I looked down at the tube-shaped object attached to a needle, static heat moved up and down my leg in frantic intensity. The corners of my vision turned white before I was immediately knocked out.

CHAPTER TWENTY-THREE

A bright light pierced my closed lids and made my headache throb with intensity. I tried to crawl to the surface of my consciousness, but each time I almost woke up, something dragged me back down the rabbit hole of my sluggish and exhausted mind.

"Ash, you've got to wake up," a voice pleaded. The tone was familiar but echoed throughout my mind in a dizzying manner that made me nauseous and confused.

"Please, Ash. Please. Wake up!" The voice shouted with an intensifying anger that shook me. Pain radiated throughout my leg, and I felt ice cold fingers on my stiff neck.

A hot slap from an open-palm gave me the last

bit of energy I needed to pull myself out of the nothingness. My cheek stung with the impact, and a disconnected cry rung out from my cracked lips.

"Ash, we've got to go," the voice said. I opened my eyes and my blurred vision revealed Josiah's hazy outline. "Ash, if we don't leave now you'll be stuck here," he pleaded while rubbing my cheek where he slapped me awake.

"Stop touching her," someone groaned beside me, and I turned to see Patrick struggling against clear chains that kept him firmly bolted against a thick metal wall.

"I have to get her out of here, Lackley will be back any second," Josiah said while punching a code into a lock and releasing the cuffs from my raw and bloody wrists.

"She's not going anywhere with you," Patrick groaned while kicking Huxley next to him, trying to wake him up. Patrick had a black eye and his shirt was bloodied.

"Jo, what's going on?" I asked. My voice sounded foreign in my ears. It felt like sandpaper was rubbing against my vocal chords. Instead of answering me, he jolted from his spot and walked over to the door. After peering outside, he walked back over to me.

"Look, I can't help all of you but I *can* get her out

of here. You have to trust me. We don't have time," he urged. His hair was sticking straight up, as if he spent the last twenty-four hours yanking it from his skull.

"Why the fuck should we trust you?" Patrick sneered. He kicked Huxley harder, and Hux groaned. My still blurred vision saw that Hux was even more hurt than Patrick.

"Because I would do anything to keep her alive," Josiah cried out while grabbing my arm and yanking me towards the door.

I struggled against him, still feeling confused and disoriented from the drugs circulating my system.

"Just stop struggling, Ash, I'm trying to save you!" Josiah yelled.

"Well, isn't this just peculiar," a calm yet snide voice said while the main door slid opened. Emperor Lackley walked in with a sinister grin. He appraised the situation, and Josiah sighed in defeat.

"Josiah, my boy, I wasn't expecting to see you in our guests' quarters," emperorLackley said while rolling up the sleeves to his crisp white dress shirt. Josiah released his hold on my arm and slipped into a cool facade of indifference.

"Yes, well, I just assumed that the Walker was useless for what you had planned. I decided that since she was originally my property, I would just bring her back to the Stonewell Manor," Josiah explained politely. I wavered where I stood and almost fell. Emperor Lackley surprisingly grabbed my arm to steady me.

"Poor little Walker, you should have a seat," he said while guiding me to a metal chair on the opposite side of the room. Once I was sitting, he pulled a vial of antibiotic serum from his pants pocket and cleansed his hands. As if touching me was dangerous. Disgusting. Once he walked away, a guard that I didn't previously notice chained my ankles and hands to bolts on the floor.

"Josiah, I recognize that you're probably just confused. The stress of this entire ordeal has made you forget," emperorLackley said in a singsong voice while walking around the room. "I'd like to cordially remind you that you don't *own* anything. I own *everything,* and I simply let the people of this world use what I allow them to," Lackley said with a bright grin as he smoothed a gray stray hair. His proper demeanor contradicted his vicious intentions.

"I find this Walker to be somewhat useful for my purposes. She's marginally important to them, therefore, for the time being, she's important to *me* ," Lackley added while patting his frail chest.

I looked around the room and saw that Kemper was now awake and struggling against his restraints. Huxley sat silently, his eyes scanning the scene, taking in every variable.

Jacob and Cyler were still asleep, and Maverick was nowhere to be found.

Emperor Lackley answered his tablet, and I noticed that whatever was said on the other line made his easygoing smile turn hard.

"Well then, I guess we need to provide him with the proper incentive," Lackley said before tossing his tablet to the guard.

"Unchain her, please," Lackley ordered while picking his nails. "It would seem that I've already found an opportunity for you to fulfill your usefulness," Lackley said to me as his gruff guard pulled me forward. "Come with us, Josiah, I've got a job for you, too."

"Don't do anything reckless," Huxley said in an even tone as I was escorted out.

I felt hopeless and unsure of the situation while the guard guided me down a long, brightly-lit hallway. Stark white tile surrounded me, giving off a clinical feel. Josiah followed us in silence, and every time I tripped from my still sluggish movements, the guard would haul me back up, causing Josiah to let out a slight hiss.

Lackley chatted idly. "It's a beautiful day outside, Ashleigh. The sunshine feels magnificent," he said while kissing the tips of his fingers. I wondered why Lackley had a sudden interest in me, a Walker. "You know, when I told Josiah to bring you to the Capital, I really wanted to see just *how* important you were to Cyler. I was very pleased to find that you also captured Maverick's heart. It was a bit of a test, you see." My heart sank, and my shakiness no longer came from the drowsiness left behind by the drugs. It was pure terror that coursed through me now.

"Ash, I love gold. Probably more than I love my wife and three sons. But do you know what I love more than anything?" Lackley asked and looked at me pointedly, but I remained quiet. "You should speak when spoken to, Walker," he growled out when I didn't respond.

"Wh-what do you love more?" I stuttered.

"I love having power over someone," emperor-Lackley said in a bright and cheery tone, as if the content of his words weren't menacing.

Finally, after about five minutes of clumsy walk-ing, I was guided into what looked like a lab.

Computers and tables full of equipment filled every spare space. I peered around, wondering what I was doing here, when Maverick's slumped form filled my line of site.

"Oh, Mav!" I exclaimed while pulling against the guard so that I could go to him. At the sound of my voice, Maverick perked up and his brown eyes met mine.

"Bringing her here isn't going to make me work faster," he gritted out through clenched teeth. Maverick flexed his arms, and I noticed electric metal cuffs around both his wrists. They were meant to shock its wearers into submission. Some families used them on their procured Walkers to discipline them .

"I think this little Walker is *very* motivating," emperorLackley said. "Have you made any progress on the serum?"

"No. It's way too complex. It has sequences I've never heard of, and the protein particles keep mutating. I don't know what you want from me." Maverick's voice sounded hopeless, and I yearned to go to him.

"Yes, well that simply won't do," Lackley replied while putting on plastic gloves and walking over to a table. "I brought you in because my advisors said that you were one of the best scientists in the entire Empire, Maverick. If anyone could fix my little *problem,* it's you."

"There wouldn't be a problem to fix if you hadn't created Influenza X," Maverick growled with such intense fury that I almost didn't realize what he said.

"Wait, you created Influenza X?" I asked in shock. The guard behind me grabbed my shoulder and pulled me tightly against his body, reigning me in. Lackley whirled around and met my terrified stare with a cold and calculating one.

"I don't normally make it a habit to explain myself to Walkers, but I think today I can make an exception." He popped his plastic gloves, smiling at me as he walked closer. I heard Josiah cough and was reminded that he was in the room, too.

"A few decades ago, when I was just a young but ambitious congressional seat holder, I overheard a meeting where my predecessor's advisors said that our current population was unsustainable. Something had to happen, or we would all die," Lackley said in a matter of fact tone while continuing to pop his gloves.

"So I came up with a solution; I hired some mediocre scientists to create a disease and its vaccine. It was fairly easy. We simply released the sickness on the Deadlands and let it work its way to the center. The elite, or those that could afford my vaccine, survived. Those that couldn't afford it, died," emperorLackley said with a shrug. He spoke in such a methodical manner about killing millions that I had to catch my breath.

"The response was phenomenal," he continued. "Our population leveled. I let society weed out those unworthy. My small circle of colleagues praised me, and within three years I became Emperor. It's easy to gain power when you can afford it, and even easier to keep it a secret when there aren't many left to question you. It also helped that the man before me fell ill to Influenza X," Lackley said with glee.

My jaw dropped, and I gaped at him. Influenza X was a manufactured illness?

"Unfortunately, I've recently learned that our vaccine has mutated, causing the vaccine reject phenomenon. It will keep mutating until eventually everyone that received it will endure the rejection," Lackley sat down in a metal chair beside Maverick.

"But that's where this ol' boy comes in! He's going to fix everything!" Lackley patted Maverick's stiff shoulder with a grin. His white teeth blended into the brightness of the room.

"I told you, I can't—" Maverick began before Lackley slapped him across the cheek.

"Don't tell me you can't. You can, and you will. If the vaccine doesn't kill her, *I will.*"

I sucked in a breath at the severity of emperor-Lackley's threat. I was immune, therefore, I never received the vaccine, but I was still very much in danger.

"I'm trying, but your timeline is ridiculous. There is no way I can crack this in the next month," Maverick said while thrusting his thick hands into his hair.

"You'll have to," Lackley said with a smile and a shrug. "The rate of mutations is growing, as is the threat of X. People who received their vaccine ten years ago are dying," emperorLackley explained. "People are beginning to question me, and the body count is getting . . . tedious."

"How long have you known about this?" I questioned.

"Why don't you answer that one, boy?" Lackley said while motioning towards Josiah. Josiah balled his fists and looked at me with desperate, wild eyes.

"We've known for a year and a half. "

My heart thudded at this revelation.

"Josiah here has been instrumental in keeping

this little mishap under wraps, haven't you my boy?"
Emperor Lackley said.

"He makes sure no one talks about my faulty
vaccine, I make sure no one talks about how he killed
his Father. Patricide is punishable by death in our
Empire. Josiah is very motivated to do my bidding.
It's a symbiotic relationship!" Emperor Lackley
clapped his hands and stood up. I flinched at the
sound of it.

Lackley bounced on the balls of his feet and
walked with a confident sway towards me. My heart
thudded. Surely emperorLackley was wrong. Josiah
couldn't have killed his own Father.

"Ash, I—" Josiah began to explain himself, but
emperorLackley cut him off.

"Yes, yes. You killed your father 'cause I told
you to, blah blah blah," Lackley said with a wave of
his hand. "But you *wanted* to. Didn't you? You
liked being the one that ended his miserable little
life." Lackley laughed, then turned back to
Maverick.

"Where is that trial serum you made earlier?"
Emperor Lackley asked Maverick.

"I put it in the refrigerator. I haven't run any tests
or even checked for toxicity. You told me to come up
with something, so I did, but I doubt it works."

Maverick's words were rushed as he worriedly scanned the room.

"Let's test it!" Lackley said with a smile while walking towards the fridge and pulling out a tray of vials.

"It has at least forty stages to go through before it's even ready for animal trials!" Maverick yelled as emperorLackley prepared a needle and walked towards me.

"Please, please, it's not ready. I've only had a day, don't—" Maverick cried out until the guard punched him in the mouth.

"Watch his head, Number Three. We need that brain of his to work," Lackley said. He tapped the tip of the needle and a bead of liquid came out.

"Oh, pl-please!" I begged while putting my arms up to block my face. The guard behind me gripped my waist against him, and I struggled to break free from his hold. It felt like I was back at Stonewell. Hopelessly fighting against those more powerful than myself.

"Stop whining, you fool," emperorLackley said with a snarl before waltzing over to Josiah. He yanked Josiah's arm out and stuck the neon blue liquid into his protruding vein.

Josiah didn't fight emperorLackley. His eyes met

mine in severe desperation. He looked at me like someone that understood his limited mortality and wanted to burn the image of me into the last pounding breaths of his existence.

"You knew when I caught you trying to escape with her that I had to punish you, Josiah," emperor-Lackley said while sliding off his gloves and placing the now empty vial of liquid on a tray. "I simply can't tolerate keeping people around that I don't trust. It's nothing personal, boy."

"I know," Josiah said softly. The injection spot where Lackley put the serum in was turning an odd shade of green and black, his veins a purple swirl of color against his shadowy skin.

"I love you," Josiah whispered to me as the blackness of the serum spread to his neck.

"Oh Josiah," I cried out in agony. The last hateful words I said to him on our call flickered through my mind as his legs collapsed from beneath him. "Jo!" I sobbed frantically while he started convulsing. His breathing became shallow, and I pulled against the guard holding me. Pain like I've never experienced before drummed beneath my skin, burning me out of existence. My cries of distress echoed throughout the Clinic as emperor-Lackley furrowed his brow.

Josiah continued to convulse and emperorLackley punched a code on his tablet, releasing Maverick from his chains. Maverick then rushed over to Josiah and turned him on his side, just as Josiah threw up. Foam formed at his mouth. After a few moments, Josiah stopped convulsing and his breathing evened out.

"Is he going to be okay?" I asked in a whimper.

"I don't know. I don't even completely understand what he was injected with," Maverick replied while balling his fist and staring at Lackley.

"Number Three, please send someone to clean this up," he said while walking over towards Maverick. "That's your first warning. The next serum you create is going in *her*," emperorLackley said while pointing at me. "And once you've killed her, I'll bring in each member of your little makeshift family one by one until you figure it out. Get it done. Get it done *now*," he growled out while stepping over Josiah's passed-out body.

The guard and emperorLackley left and locked us in the Clinic. I kneeled by Josiah as Maverick cleaned up his vomit. Swirls of black peeked through his skin, and occasionally his face squinted in pain.

"What are we going to do?" I sobbed. Everything hit me at once, and despite wanting to be strong and hold my emotions together, I couldn't help but shake with fear and distress over all that had been revealed to me.

"You've all received the vaccine, haven't you?" I asked, fearing the answer.

"All but Kemper. He's immune," Maverick said in a sad voice.

Everyone I knew and cared about was in danger.

CHAPTER TWENTY-FOUR

I spent the next hour wiping Josiah's brow. Sticky sweat rolled down his face, and he alternated between shivers and shouts of pain.

Maverick ran a multitude of tests on the central computer to see what within his trial serum was causing such a horrible reaction.

"I don't even know where to begin looking, Ash," he said in a defeated tone while typing furiously on the keyboard. "I don't know if he needs a cure, or if this will run its course. I don't know if I created a brand new fucking disease!" Maverick screamed while thrusting a fist on the keyboard, causing it to break.

I ran to him and wrapped my arms around Maverick's back. He shook with unshed tears and the punches he couldn't throw. "We can do this, Mav. I hate to say this, but your priority is going to have to be fixing the vaccine. Jo seems to be okay." He was currently curled up in the fetal position, clutching his stomach as he slept. "I think I can take care of him while you work on the serum," I said, even though it felt like daggers in my gut to even consider not doing everything in my power to save Josiah. There were too many unknowns. Despite everything, I knew that prioritizing the greater good had to take precedence. We couldn't sacrifice all for one.

"Ash, I would never do anything to hurt you. If I had known for one second he was going to inject Josiah with that, I wouldn't have even made it. I felt pressured and just threw something together to make him happy," Maverick said while thrusting his hand into his hair and closing his eyes.

"I know, I know. We can grieve and cry and cuss later, right now we have a job to do. What do you need from me?" I asked in a surprisingly calm tone. Every fiber of my existence wanted to break apart into despair, but a mature determination wove its way around my heart, numbing the pain until I could process it all.

"Take care of Josiah and look for a way out of

here. I'll be able to focus once I know that they aren't threatening you," Maverick whispered while covering his mouth and looking intently into the corner.

I saw a blinking camera fixed on us and nodded in understanding.

Maverick looked at me like there was an ocean between us. I wanted to swim across it to make sure we were okay, that somehow we would figure it out.

"Make sure you keep his fever down. Keep him cool with wet rags. Let me know if he starts showing any new symptoms or if the black poison marks spread anymore," he said, looking at Josiah with an expression of pure guilt. My heart broke for Maverick. He truly valued all life.

Maverick dove into work, and I spent the day logging any and all changes within Josiah. He slept the entire time, but I noticed that his eyes moved rapidly beneath his closed lids. He no longer had a fever, but still emitted sharp grunts of pain occasionally while clutching his stomach.

A guard brought us lunch, but Maverick didn't stop to eat. I watched as he fluttered frantically between his microscope and the computer. He muttered to himself and took notes now and then. I kept reticent. I learned from our mornings together at the Clinic that Maverick needed silence to work proficiently.

Three days passed in the same way. I looked after a deteriorating Josiah while Maverick worked himself thin. When he wasn't reconstructing the makeup of the faulty X vaccine, he was analyzing blood samples from Josiah. He only slept briefly. We didn't talk much, for fear of being overheard. We were trapped in an unwinnable scenario.

On the fourth day, it was eerily silent. The door opened mid-morning, which was unusual for the guard schedule. I covered Josiah with a towel and turned to face whatever brutal mind games emperor-Lackley threw at us next but was incredibly surprised to see a nervous-looking guard. He eyed the camera in the corner of the room then quickly motioned for me to come closer.

Maverick, who hadn't even noticed that someone had entered the lab, was trying to stay awake while observing a gene sequence in a vaccine reject's blood sample.

"Can I help you?" I asked while mentally kicking myself. I sounded like I was back in the Stonewell Manor.

The guard widened his eyes then looked back at the camera. He oozed tension and fear.

Once I was close enough, the guard grabbed my hand and dropped a note into my palm before whispering, "Tell Tallis to let my sister go. I did what he asked." My chest heaved in shock. Tallis had his sister?

I nodded yes insistently, and the Guard ran out of the room after glancing down at Josiah with a look of pity in his eyes. I clutched at the note in my palm and nonchalantly turned my back to the camera, ensuring that my hands were hidden from its sight. Taking a deep breath, I opened my hand and smoothed out the crumpled note before reading it.

We're coming for you. Unscrew the vent in your room. Tell Maverick to hack the central air unit and turn off the main fan. One hour.

I nearly dropped the note, then checked the clock. I couldn't leave within the hour. Josiah wasn't up for travel. I made my way over to Maverick and tentatively put a hand on his shoulder, which caused him to jump. I casually eyed the camera which made Maverick squint his eyes in curiosity and stand up. I wrapped my arms around him and nuzzled into his chest so that no one could hear me or read my lips.

"Tallis is coming for us. He needs you to hack the central air unit and turn off the main fan," I whispered. Maverick tensed, and for a brief moment, I wondered if he heard me.

"Okay," he said before letting me go to return to his computer.

I made my way towards the far wall where the giant vent was located and propped up a chair behind me to inconspicuously hide what I was doing. Then, I used the tips of my nails to unscrew the small metal screws from the vent face to the wall. My nails bled, but I continued working on unscrewing the vent, only stopping to wipe my hands on my dress.

"Josiah doesn't seem to be doing well," Maverick said loudly, and I stopped my work to turn quickly and check on Josiah. He wasn't doing well, but his condition hadn't worsened. "I think he'll need to stay here and rest under observation for at least a week; I hope they don't move him," Maverick added, and I immediately understood what he was trying to say. Josiah couldn't come with us. Once Tallis got here, Maverick and I would have to leave without him.

I wriggled the last screw loose, then went over to Josiah. I had about fifteen minutes left before Tallis would be here, according to his note. I placed my hand on Josiah's forehead and sighed. I spent a lifetime worrying, loving, and caring for this man. There was so much pain. So much dysfunction and unanswered questions still. Did he kill his Father?

Despite all of this, my heart broke at the unknown. I knew that this could very well be my last moment with Josiah. I knew that the odds of him surviving were slim, and it felt like a boulder was breaking through my numb barriers and making me feel an onslaught of fear and grief.

I leaned down and whispered into Josiah's unconscious ear. "Josiah, nothing about this is right," I began. "I'm not sure what hurts more; the pain of all that's happened between us, or the ache of what never will be," I choked out as a single tear danced down my cheek. I reached out and grabbed his clammy hand. "All my life, I admired you, Jo, and I think admiration is as close to love as we ever got. Please get better."

I didn't say goodbye to Josiah, but I felt him squeeze my hand. It was our last unrequited conversation. The last one-sided piece of affection I'd ever give him.

The minutes of the clock clicked by as Maverick's exhausted fingers typed away tirelessly. "I shut it off, they should be here any second," Maverick whispered. I expected a huge commotion or war to erupt, but instead, to my surprise, Jules slinked through the opening of the vent wearing an all-black, leather suit that looked identical to Mia's usual get up.

She waltzed through like she owned the place, and I frantically waved and pointed at the camera flashing in the corner.

"Oh, don't worry, we interrupted the feed ages ago, Lackley is mighty cocky, this was easy," Jules said while slumping down in a chair and picking her nails as if she made it a habit climbing through the Emperor's vents on rescue missions. But there was a slight tremor in her voice, and her eyes shifted around the room. Josiah grunted, and she peered at him with diluted concern.

"He looks like shit." She scrunched up her face in disgust. "You all ready to go? We have about ten minutes till guard shift change," she said nonchalantly.

Maverick and I exchanged curious glances. Surely it couldn't be *that* easy .

"Tallis is getting the guys, we need to go soon," she said while standing up, stretching, and sauntering over to the vent.

"How did you even—" I began before she cut me off.

"Oh, little Walker. Can we talk about this later?"

Jules asked in a patronizing tone. "My brother looks like he's about to do something heroic and stupid, so I suggest you use the next sixty seconds to talk him out of it, so we can get the fuck out of here. I'll be in the air duct."

I whirled around and peered at Maverick. He looked like he swallowed a porcupine. "Ash, I'm staying here," he said while walking towards me.

"No, you aren't," I replied simply. "Aren't you the one that always calls me on my martyr act? You're not staying here. End of discussion." I crossed my arms over my chest. Maverick grasped my elbows and yanked them from me. He folded my arms around his waist and pulled me close.

"Emperor Lackley is crazy, but his lab is far superior to mine. I need to stay behind and figure this out. There are a lot of lives on the line. Plus, someone needs to keep an eye on Josiah," Maverick added. We both turned to look at Jo, who was heaving deep breaths. It looked like he just sprinted a mile.

"What if Lackley punishes you for my escape?" I questioned while looking back at the clock with tears in my eyes. Jules said a minute which meant I had twenty seconds to convince him to come with us.

"Lackley won't punish me, he needs me." Mav began rubbing small circles on my back. "Once you get the rest of the guys out, they'll find a way to get to me. Until then, it'll give me more time to crack this mutation and look over Jo."

I felt a massive sense of regret build beneath my skin. I needed more time. Maybe it was the pressure of the last few days or the fear of never seeing him again, but I tentatively raised up on my tiptoes and brushed my lips against Maverick's. I refused to let another moment go by without allowing him to know just how much he meant to me .

At first, he was tentative; his lips moved cautiously against mine as if he was afraid I would break under the pressure building between us. But then he leaned over more, and we met in the middle of fear and wistful promises. Our kiss was like a wave. It crashed to the shore, and we wanted to walk along its intensity before the ocean claimed it back. This wasn't the last time I'd see Maverick. This wasn't the end of our story.

Maverick's lips trailed along my jaw and towards my neck. His exploratory kisses ended just at my ear, and I felt the flick of his tongue before he whispered against me, "Your kiss tastes like the rest of my life." He hummed out a low baritone moan. "I can guarantee that I'll see you again. Go, before I change my mind and do what I *want* to do instead of what I need to."

I made my way over to the air duct, not caring that my first kiss with Maverick was in the Emperor's lab with Josiah and Jules, or that thousands of lives were in his capable hands. Before entering the duct where an angry Jules sat impatiently, I turned around and saw Maverick loosen his tie and clench his jaw. His fists were balled, and I wondered if he, too, was struggling to keep still, to not forget the world and the heavy weight upon our shoulders.

"Bye," I mouthed. *I love you* , I thought.

CHAPTER TWENTY-FIVE

I struggled to keep up with Jules as her slinky movements navigated the tight, humid air ducts with ease. Occasionally, she referenced her watch for directions, but otherwise, she appeared to be confident in her directional capabilities. Never in my wildest dreams would I have imagined that it would be Jules to head up my rescue mission. Although I was learning that Jules was made up of many parts, some good, some bad, I didn't necessarily trust her not to lose me within the complex ventilation system.

A massive fan at the end of the duct was stationary, and we snaked our way through its dusty wide-set blades and out another vent. The crawl space was small and suffocating, and I briefly wondered how the guys were going to fit through the duct. Once outside, Jules placed a perfectly manicured finger to her peach lips and crouched low. It was dark out, and the air smelled of pinewoods with the hint of burning plastic. The static in the air made my hair frizz. We crawled towards a waiting transport cloaked in darkness about five hundred feet away.

Once the door slid open and we were safely inside, the empty transport took off. "Where is everyone?" I asked, but Jules stayed quiet. She studied the dash and adjusted the settings while inputing our destination. She furrowed her arched brow in seriousness and kept looking out the windows to ensure we weren't followed. Something wasn't right.

"Jules, what's going on," I whispered while entertaining the notion of jumping out of the moving transport and escaping whatever Jules had up her sleeve. Where was Tallis? Where were the guys?

"Tallis is at a non-disclosed meeting point seventy miles outside of the Confederation of Dasos," Jules said quietly. She didn't meet my eyes as she gathered her hair into a messy bun on top of her head. Thick black tendrils fell in her eyes, and she brushed them away.

"Will the guys and Mia meet us there?" I asked. I felt eager to see them and devise a rescue mission for Maverick.

"No," Jules replied in a tight voice that made my stomach drop.

"They couldn't fit through the duct, Ashleigh. Anyone with half a brain could have inferred that. I can't believe you just thought we could magically rescue them; you're lucky you made it out of there alive," Jules chided with a grin while picking at the black paint on her nails. "Tallis wanted Mia to stay behind; he said she had some fucked up code of honor shit to fulfill. Maverick promised me the job at the schoolhouse if I agreed to help, so here we are." Jule's words crushed me. I had unknowingly left them all there. What sort of fate would meet them?

"We have to go back," I immediately urged.

"For once, I agree with you. I might not like them right now, but I don't want to see them die. Besides, I'm in no position to run a Providence, and if anything happened to Cyler or Maverick, I'd have to take over Dormas. But we can't go back today," Jules said with an air of selfishness and finality.

"Jules, certainly we can—" I began.

"We can't get them, Ash!" she screamed. Her face slipped into a tidal wave of emotions. "They're stuck there until we can come up with a better plan! For some reason, Maverick made your safety a priority, and if I have any hopes of getting in their good graces again, I have to respect that. I hate this. I hate all of this," she cried out while punching the glass window, then rubbing her throbbing fist.

I froze in my seat and watched as each facet of Jules came into place. She was suffering, and I completely saw her as the woman she was—Broken.

"I just want my life back." Jules shook with intensity as she resumed picking the paint off her nails. "Did Jacob tell you all that happened that day?" she asked, and I shook my head no. I had a general idea but that was it.

"When I turned fifteen, Cyler and Maverick sent me away to school in Galla. I went home for the summer. After being gone for eight months. Eight. Months. Jacob was the only one that greeted me at the train station." She paused, and I briefly wondered why she was revealing this to me. "I've always loved Jacob, and when I saw that it was only him there, I thought, 'Surely this is it -- he loves me too.' " Jules let soft tears run down her face, and black makeup smeared along her cheeks and beneath her eyes. "I kissed him, but he pushed me away," she choked out while touching her soft finger tips to her lips, as if remembering the sensation of Jacob. "Then I ran to the manor but was greeted with confused expressions. Maverick and

Cy forgot that I was coming home. Forgot about *me*.
"

"Jules, I— "

"Don't interrupt me."

She stretched her legs out while adjusting her clothes. "They saw me crying, and when they asked what was wrong, I don't know what came over me. It just *slipped*. I was so hurt by Jacob, and so mad at my family, that I blurted out that ridiculous excuse. Maverick and Cy didn't buy it for a minute. But I didn't account for Huxley and the demons that plagued him. So when Jacob walked through the door, Huxley went wild. I—I've never seen anything like it. I was so frozen in fear that I couldn't get the words out. Couldn't admit to my lie."

I didn't know what to say. I lacked the words to adequately express the sadness I felt. I wanted to fix all their problems. I wanted Jules to find a way back into their family dynamic.

"I'm not telling you this for your pity, Walker. Wipe your eyes," she growled, and I immediately began cleaning my face of the tears that fell. "I need you to know that I'll do anything to fix this, and if that means rescuing a little Walker whore, then so be it."

"Jules, how did Maverick get in contact with

you?" I questioned. Jules squirmed in discomfort, and I knew a change in subject was necessary.

"Mav sent a one-way distress signal," she replied while wiping snot and salty tears from her red face. "Tallis was with Claude when Lackley's street team ambushed you. He called me the moment he realized Claude sold you out," Jules began

"Claude sold us out?" I replied in shock.

"That slimy asshole sent word to Lackley's men the first chance he got," Jules said with disgust. "Luckily, Tallis took care of him, the rat bastard," Jules said with a hint of wistfulness. "Tallis was able to get a guard to give us blueprints of the building, as well as get a message back to you. Maverick followed through on his side of the plan and gave Tallis implicit instructions not to let you know that they were planning on staying behind, as well as guaranteed that my transgressions would be forgiven if I helped."

I cursed. Maverick was in serious trouble.

"Jules, stop the transport," I asserted in a firm voice.

"NO!" Jules howled in response. I racked my brain for options, but each thought fell short.

"Reroute us for the city-center. We can wait this out and try again," I pleaded.

"I don't think you heard me, Ash! Maverick promised that I could stop working in the gardens as well as have my crimes against Jacob forgiven. You can bet your little Walker ass that I'm not going to let you ruin that for me with some shitty attempt at a rescue," Jules lectured.

I placed my head in my hands and continued to brainstorm .

"Ash, I'd rather claw my eyes out with a rusty spoon than work with you, but I know when to tap out and regroup," Jules said in an oddly mature sentiment.

I didn't want to admit out loud that Jules was right. I cursed my Walker upbringing. What use were cooking skills and household training when the ones you cared for needed a warrior? I released the notion that we could somehow magically invade the Emperor's Lab to rescue them unscathed and agreed to reassemble then come up with a plan.

We traveled in silence, aside from the occasional huff from Jules. The further from everyone we got, the more my heart felt like lead. Worry threaded through the gaps in my soul, binding me together in a ball of anxiety and angst. Were we doing the right thing? Could I have done better?

"Isn't it peculiar how things never change?" Jules

asked. She appeared calmer now, as she held her fingers against her forehead near the bridge of her nose.

"What do you mean?" I asked.

"I've chased those boys around since I was in diapers. I never once caught up. Even now, I'm chasing after their ghosts," Jules spoke with such a calm sadness that I worried for her sanity.

"I don't hate you because you're a Walker. Or even because you're ignorant and naive about this world. I hate you because you so effortlessly slipped into their group," Jules said while removing her hand from her face then slumping in her seat. She gave me a cold, calculating gaze. I thought of Jacob, he truly did care for Jules. I saw it in the way he agonized over his relationship with her. How he wished he saw her the way she saw him.

"Jacob cares for y—" I began.

"Don't you say his name to me! Don't pretend to know him better than I do. Jacob was the only one that let me in. I loved him," she rushed out, her words flowing in manic worry.

"Do you still love him?" I asked, I needed to know. I craved to understand their dynamic .

"I stopped loving Jacob when I almost killed him. A love like that is too destructive," she replied, and I agreed. Unrequited love made even the best of people toxic and bitter.

WE MADE our way towards an abandoned building with boarded up windows and trash scattered along its red-brick exterior. I recognized that we were in one of the many towns that died when X hit, and I noticed a rusted sign that indicated the city was called Tombstone; a fitting name for such a ghostly place. We stopped the transport, and Jules cloaked the outside so that no one could easily find us. We made our way inside the abandoned building and were greeted with dusty mismatched furniture, rat droppings, and the smell of rotted food. Once Tallis saw us, he waltzed forward and grabbed Jules' face. She looked distressed, and he examined every square inch of her.

"I'm fine, no need to make a big production of it," she snarled in response, causing Tallis to smirk then look at me.

"It pleases me to see that you both survived the trip," he said in his smoky voice. I noticed how close he stood to Jules.

"Please tell me you have a plan to get them back, Tallis," I begged while pinching my thigh through the thick material of my Galla-style dress. I felt dirty and exhausted but was eager to rescue my guys, now. I lacked the know-how as well as the training to ambush a heavily guarded facility, but I felt reckless and desperate. I wanted my family back.

"I have a plan, but you're not going to like it," Tallis said while rolling up his sleeves, revealing his forearms. I noticed Jules swallow in appreciation. There was definitely something between them. I could almost feel the sparks cracking throughout the room. "Maverick briefly explained emperorLackley's purpose for abducting them, and I think our best move is to let the rest of the world know," Tallis explained. He poured me a glass of water and handed it to me .

"Who is going to believe a Walker and a Scavenger?" Jules scoffed while crossing her arms and rolling her eyes. "If emperorLackley even thinks there's a rebellion on his doorstep, he'll go on a killing spree."

"I don't think so. I think he'll be too busy worrying about the mass of people wanting to kill him," Tallis said with a mischievous grin. "And it won't be a Walker and a Scavenger telling the world, it will be the beautiful, tear-stained face of Cyler and Maverick Black's baby sister," Tallis said with a smirk.

"You want to put my face on a rebellion?" Jules shrieked, evidently not fond of this idea.

"It'll provide the distraction we need to keep emperorLackley busy; it might even get him killed, there will be a lot of angry people at his doorstep. Once all hell breaks loose we'll swoop in to rescue them," Tallis argued.

"I . . . don't think I'm the right person to do this," Jules countered. I watched their battle with interest.

Tallis moved even closer to Jules, and I blushed at the intensity that burned between them. "If you want to be the person you're destined to become, you must decide on what kind of person you want to be, *Agapimenos.*" The nickname rolled off his tongue, and I wondered what it meant. "*You* are the person that's going to be strong and stand up for what's right. *You* are going to save your family," he whispered. Jules' eyes wavered in exhaustion.

"I don't want to be anything," Jules argued. "I'm here to get my life back."

"Whatever you say," Tallis replied with a knowing grin as if he saw Jules as wholly for the broken, grieving mess she truly was.

"Fine, so, what now?" Jules questioned while shrugging off Tallis' intense gaze.

"Now we tell the world," I answered, and both of them turned towards me.

JULES BRUSHED her hair but didn't remove the evidence of her tears; she smudged dirt creatively on her cheek that made her look like she just came out of battle. Tallis was right, Jules was dramatic and manipulative enough to pull this off. The entire Empire would feel sympathetic towards her.

I made quick work of manufacturing a dark backdrop to our video, furthering the dismal tone we wanted to evoke. "You'll need to show fierce anger while juggling vulnerability, *Agapimenos* ," Tallis said while getting his tablet ready.

"Whatever," Jules replied. Fear rippled through her facade.

I wondered if we could pull this off, if she would be strong enough to tell the world of emperorLackley's evil past and inspire the world to take revenge. Tallis noticed her fear, too, and he eyed her before smiling mischievously. He waltzed over to her with determined strides, grabbed her face, and then kissed her. *Hard.* She rose up on her tiptoes to meet the force of his crushing kiss. After a brief moment, I realized I was staring at their passionate display, so I coughed and averted my eyes.

Tallis walked back over towards me while licking his lips. He looked ruffled and winked at me before ordering "And, NOW," while turning on the tablet.

"Masters and Mistresses of the Empire," Jules began. "I am Jules Black, sister of Maverick and Cyler Black, the humble and kind leaders of Dormas. I come to you from a hiding post within the Empire." She looked down at her arm before dramatically raising her chin and giving an icy glare to Tallis who was behind the camera. "I have recently learned some grave news that could impact the very fabric of our Empire's existence. In a drastic and inhumane attempt at controlling our population, emperor-Lackley commissioned the creation of Influenza X. He is responsible for the murder of our friends, our brothers, our sisters, our parents, and our neighbors. He destroyed entire cities. Enslaved the peoples of this empire with his vaccine. Divided our Empire. Broke our families. Killed our loved ones. emperor-Lackley is a murderer and a fraud," Jules proclaimed. Goosebumps erupted on my arms.

"People of the Empire, emperorLackley must be stopped. He recently learned that his precious vaccine is malfunctioning, so now he is holding my brilliant, helpless brother and the rest of the Dormas leaders hostage in a vicious attempt to further his powerful reign and control us. I implore you. Help me save my brothers. Help me save our Empire." As she ended her speech, a small, timid tear danced perfectly down her porcelain cheeks.

Tallis cut the feed then began furiously sending the video to as many contacts across the Empire as he could, praying that the announcement would go viral and we'd get reactions within twenty-four hours. Emperor Lackley had control over the airwaves, but Tallis ensured us that the video would find its way into the right hands, hands that could get Jules' speech heard.

"So, what now?" I asked.

"Now we send a message to Maverick and the others, warning them," Tallis said. Jules nodded in agreement.

"How do we do that?" I asked.

"I'll send another note through the Guard that got a note to you. He thinks I have his sister held captive; she's an old . . . uh . . . friend of mine," Tallis said while rubbing the back of his neck, causing Jules to groan.

"Disgusting," she sneered while looking at Tallis with a mixture of frustration and desire.

"I'll write the note," I replied automatically while jumping up from my seat. I was overly eager to grasp at whatever contact I could.

"Keep it ambiguous, so if intercepted we can't be traced. I can get it to him by nightfall," he added before going over to a table full of knives and sharpening them.

M,

The rest of your life starts tomorrow.

— A

EPILOGUE

Kemper

The fluorescent light in the right corner of our makeshift jail cell kept flickering in a systematic sequence. If my right eye wasn't swollen shut, and my left not blurred from all the rogue punches I just endured, maybe I could make sense of them. We kept pushing the boundaries of the Guards. Spitting in their eyes. Kicking them during bathroom breaks. In turn, they kept pushing back. Just enough to keep us hurting and down.

Perhaps I was grasping for straws. Trying to find a pattern where there wasn't one. But sitting here while Ash and Maverick were off in danger made me desperate to make sense of something. Anything.

Cyler groaned out. "How long do you think it's been?"

"Ten days and six hours. Give or take," I replied instantly. I counted the seconds between guard shift-changes and determined that we got a new guard every four hours.

"Do we have a plan yet?" Huxley asked.

We both eyed our snoozing guard. His over-grown belly made his weapon belt look like twine tightly wound on raw meat. He would be easy to take down.

Hux was probably the most beat up out of all of us. He needed medical attention soon. Kicking a guard in the groin would do that. My eye drifted to the flashing light again. On. Off. On on. Off.

"Mia," I began. She had been meditating in eerie silence since our capture, only speaking up to yell at us when we talked about escaping. "Does that light flashing seem strange to you?" She casually looked at the light, and I saw her busted lip grin.

"It's Morse code. Some of the tribes use it. Someone must be trying to send a message," Mia said methodically.

"Well, what does it say?!" Jacob pleaded. He was the least calm out of all of us. I noticed blood seeping down his hands from his rubbed-raw wrists.

"A—S—H—I—S—S—A—F—E—" Mia spelled out slowly. "Well fuck, they could have at least told us a way to get out of here," she joked. The rest of us, even Huxley, collectively sighed in relief. The only person smart enough to hack into the light controls would be Maverick. Leave it to him to come up with a way to communicate with us using a language only Scavengers understood.

"At least you know lover girl is safe," Mia said with a sigh before closing her eyes and going back into her meditative state. I wondered how she kept so calm. How she could just sit there.

"Thank God for that," I muttered as Patrick groaned while spitting up blood. I'm pretty sure he bit the hell out of his tongue when the last guard punched him in the jaw.

"For the record, when we get out of here, I'm courting her," I said definitively. I wasn't dancing around this anymore. Ash deserved to be loved and cherished. I wasn't going to waste another second not doing so.

"Get in line, Kemp," Patrick chuckled.

"So we're doing this? Really doing this?" Jacob asked. I knew that he would be the least secure out of all of us in this new adventure. We'd have to make sure we were careful. Intentional.

"We're doing this," Cyler answered firmly.

We all remained silent, waiting for Huxley to speak up. To confirm what we already knew .

"Do we have to talk about this right now?" Hux complained.

"Yes or no, Hux. It's not that fucking hard," Patrick said through clenched teeth, shocking us all. He was the last person I'd ever expect to force Hux into deciding.

"Shut up!" Mia yelled, and the authority of it shocked us into silence. I had almost forgot she was here with us. "Hear that boys?" Mia asked with a grin. I strained to listen but heard nothing. "A bomb just hit the north corner of the building, and sirens are going off in the East wing," she murmured while closing her eyes.

"How can you even hear that? This room is concrete!" Patrick exclaimed.

"I've got good ears," she replied with a shrug. "And while you were comparing dick sizes and fighting about whether or not you're going to court Ash, *I* was conserving energy and figuring out a way to get out of this hell hole."

I strained my ear to hear what she was talking about. A faint, low boom erupted, and I widened my eyes in surprise. She was right. Something was happening. I looked up at the flashing light and saw that it had taken on a new sequence.

"Mia—quick. What is the light saying now?" I asked.

Jacob started rubbing against his chains again.

"G—E—T—O—U—T—N—O—W," she spelled out. "Well boys, what do you say we jump this joint?" Mia shimmied out of her cuffs with ease, and if my eyes weren't swollen and my head wasn't throbbing, I would have thrown her an incredulous look.

"How?" Cyler asked while she uncuffed him using the guard's tablet.

"No time, let's get the fuck out of here," Mia said before hitting the snoozing guard across the head with a pipe and stealing his electric gun.

We shuffled down the hall on high alert. I could now hear an alarm going off in the distance as the lights overhead flickered. I sniffed and noticed that the air smelled like an electrical fire and a hint of burnt plastic .

"We don't even know where we're going," Jacob complained. His broad hands touched the ceramic-tiled walls, as if trying to prevent them from closing in on him.

"We follow the sounds of the bombs," Mia whispered. "Where there are bombs, there's bound to be a hole in the wall—an opening to get out of here," she explained.

"Sound logic, but where there are bombs, there's also—well—*bombs* ," Cyler bit out sarcastically. I think he hated that he didn't have all the answers this time.

Huxley coughed, and I noticed blood splatter on his arm and clothes. Fuck. We needed to get him to a doctor. We turned the corner, following Mia's intuition as to where we should go.

"Where are the guards?" Huxley whispered while crouching low and clutching his stomach.

"Probably all responding to the bombs on the other side of the building," I suggested.

"Surely there would be some sort of commotion? Someone here?" Patrick asked.

"It's like they all abandoned this place," Huxley said with a furrowed brow before covering his mouth.

We were all conditioned to know that abandoned places meant disease. Meant X.

We made a sharp turn left at the end of the hall and the lights went out. My vision was already bad, but now I felt defenseless. The only guide I had was Mia's labored breathing as she led us. I took small steps.

"Maverick?" Mia's voice whisper-shouted. "Is that you? Why are you holding a body?" she asked, and the world as I knew it collapsed.

Ash. Oh god what happened to Ash? I wanted to crumble to the ground. I wanted to murder Lackley. I felt Huxley tense beside me, and Jacob sucked in a breath. All I could think of was all the time I wasted.

"It's Josiah," Maverick's low voice scratched out. A brief, blinding relief consumed me. "Look, I don't have time to explain. Ash is safe with Tallis. We need to get out of here. He's lost use of his legs . . ." he trailed off.

"Just fucking leave him here," Huxley said incredulously before checking my shoulder and walking ahead of us.

"I'll help you," I said to Maverick, and together we continued towards the bombs. I wanted to leave Josiah behind, too, but knew Maverick probably had a good reason for bringing him.

A bright light at the end of the darkened hallway acted like a beacon to us. White smoke and zipping fuses blasted around us. I kept straining to hear the sound of footsteps, but there were none. We were all that was left. As we walked I noticed something like sand on the floor, with bits and pieces of clothing. Surely we weren't . . . .

"Heat. Whoever is out there fucking has Heat, look," Cyler said incredulously while bending down and grasping a handful of sand. It seeped through his fingers. We were shuffling through powdered, dead bodies.

I shivered as I covered my mouth to prevent the kicked-up dust from getting in my lungs. Slowly, ever so slowly, we slunk along the wall towards the new entrance to the building.

"Come on out, boys!" a sharp, masculine voice called to us.

We deliberated for a moment. No weapons. No clue where we were. No clue how to get the hell out of here. I readjusted Josiah's passed-out body on my shoulder and winced at the pain in my side.

Normally we would have debated on the situation and come up with a plan, but Mia had other ideas. She simply smoothed out her pants and sashayed out through the cracked opening in the building.

"Boys, huh?" she asked with a coy smile. "Now I'm offended. It was a *girl* that saved their asses," she yelled out while putting her hands up in surrender. We all stayed behind, listening for any indication that it was safe. I felt totally emasculated letting Mia take charge, but all of us were beat to hell and useless in a fight. After what felt like hours, Mia's face flashed in the opening, startling us all.

"Fuck, Mia! Warn a guy!" Huxley exclaimed. I tried not to grin at the fact that something rattled him
.

"Come out, you're gonna want to see this. *Agrio* got us an army!" Mia pranced off, as if she didn't just spend ten days in captivity.

Slowly we all made our way out, and the sight that greeted us was nothing short of amazing. Bright orange and black striped flags waved in the wind around us, and underneath their glory stood about a hundred Ethros warriors. A tall man with bronze skin and a wired mustache walked towards us. He was decked out in an orange cotton uniform with black medals covering his chest.

"Well, hello there!" he said with a head nod. "I'm Commodore Sebastian Cavil," he introduced himself, outstretching his hand with a smile. None of us took it. Ethros is where Cyler and Patrick were headed when emperorLackley abducted them. We spent our time in captivity assuming Ethros leaked intel.

"Ah, I see you don't trust us quite yet. Understandable. Perhaps you'll trust us after you see your Ash? Hmm?" He gestured behind him where one of the soldiers wearing an all-orange jumpsuit was taking off his hat and walking towards us. Long white hair fell around his face. Tallis.

"Tallis, what's going on? Is Ash with you? What about Jules?" Maverick growled out. Usually it was Cyler that negotiated trade deals and alliances, but I saw him struggling to stand. Blood had gathered in his mouth.

I started to slip under the weight of Josiah's body, and we slowly lowered him to the dirt ground before I moved to Cyler and helped him sit. Tallis shook Mav's hand with a smile.

"Ash and Jules are in a safe house outside the city. I figured you wouldn't appreciate me bringing them to a battle," Tallis explained with a grin. *Thank God.*

Commodore observed us with a smile. He looked power hungry and volatile. "And, to answer your question, Maverick. We're here to take over the Empire."

ACKNOWLEDGMENTS

I would like to express my gratitude to the many people who saw me through this book; to all those who provided support, talked things over, read, wrote, offered comments, and assisted in the editing, proofreading and design. My editors, Jenifer Knox and Michelle Hoffman. Beta Readers, Mads, Ellen, Gabrielle, Rachal, Helayna, and Luiza. My Mom, Jennifer, who provided support and a little tough love when needed. Above all, I want to thank my husband, Josh, and the rest of my family who support and encourage me in spite of all the time this journey takes me away from them.

ABOUT THE AUTHOR

CoraLee June has always been passionate about storytelling and impressed by the influence it has on people and the decisions they make in life. She loves engaging with the projects she works on, diving headfirst into developing real, raw, and relatable characters that are equally flawed and beautiful. CoraLee lives in Dallas, Tx with her husband and two daughters. She's been known to frequently indulge in boxed red wine and day-old pizza. When she's not writing, June is reading or substitute teaching at the local middle school.

For more information and bonus scenes subscribe to my blog at

www.authorcoraleejune.com

AuthorCoraleeJune@Gmail.com

Heart of the Walker

Fight of the Walker

Soul of the Elite